25 ROSES

Also by Stephanie Faris

30 Days of No Gossip

25 ROSES

STEPHANIE FARIS

ALADDIN

NEW YORK   LONDON   TORONTO   SYDNEY   NEW DELHI

ALADDIN

An imprint of Simon & Schuster Children's Publishing Division

1230 Avenue of the Americas, New York, New York 10020

First Aladdin hardcover edition January 2015

Text copyright © 2015 by Stephanie Faris

Jacket illustration copyright © 2015 by Adrian Valencia

Also available in an Aladdin M!X paperback edition.

All rights reserved, including the right of reproduction in whole or in part in any form.

ALADDIN is a trademark of Simon & Schuster, Inc., and related logo is a registered trademark of Simon & Schuster, Inc.

For information about special discounts for bulk purchases, please contact Simon & Schuster Special Sales at 1-866-506-1949 or business@simonandschuster.com.

The Simon & Schuster Speakers Bureau can bring authors to your live event. For more information or to book an event contact the Simon & Schuster Speakers Bureau at 1-866-248-3049 or visit our website at www.simonspeakers.com.

Book designed by Laura Lyn DiSiena

The text of this book was set in Minion Pro.

Manufactured in the United States of America 1214 FFG

10 9 8 7 6 5 4 3 2 1

Library of Congress Control Number 2014943723

ISBN 978-1-4814-3133-0 (hc)

ISBN 978-1-4814-2420-2 (pbk)

ISBN 978-1-4814-2421-9 (eBook)

For my mother, Valerie Walton.
Everything I am today, I owe to you.

25 ROSES

CHAPTER ONE

❤

To: Stanton Middle School
From: Mia Hartley
This place could use a real-life Cupid.

I don't ask for much on a Tuesday morning. A ride to school without listening to my big sister Kellie gabbing on the phone with her BFF, Margeaux. Maybe a few minutes where Mom actually listens to me instead of Kellie. Oh, and extra room in the backseat to set a box full of notecards to attach to chocolate roses so I don't have to hold it in my lap all the way to school.

Unfortunately, none of those things were happening. My sister was doing the whole, "And then I said, and then she said" thing while my mom ignored my questions about dropping me off at school first. The cards in the box on my lap had to be filled out for our Valentine's Day sale, which was a huge deal in my school every year. I'd been selling roses for a week. Today was the last day.

Why did I have the box? Blame it on my desire to be liked. I signed up to help sell these because my BFF wanted to do it. And because if you did things like this, people knew who you were. It was nicer than being invisible, I figured.

Why was the box on my lap? Good question. Because my cheerleader-slash-homecoming-attendant-slash-most-popular-sophomore-at-Stanton-High-School sister had to have a place for her stupid science project. Which she'd probably get an A-plus-plus on because, in case it wasn't obvious, she's perfect—the golden child.

I, meanwhile, have never gotten a carnation, a rose, or even a pile of fake doody from a boy. Today my best friend, Ashleigh, and I would sell chocolate roses before school. Then tomorrow—Valentine's Day—we'd hand those roses out in homeroom. That was when things would *really* get boring.

If this year was the same as last year, we'd take orders for cards, only to find they were all for the same eight people. But this year, instead of watching other people hand out the cards, it would be me and Ashleigh. We'd have to pass out roses to those same eight people while people like me,

Ashleigh, and most of the rest of seventh grade would be left sitting there, looking like nobodies.

"*Mia!*"

Kellie was yelling at me from the front seat. "What?" I asked loudly. If she was going to yell, I was going to yell too.

"You'll be at the game Friday night, right?"

I frowned and wrinkled my nose. It was an automatic reaction to her "game requests." If Kellie had been looking at me, she would have been mad. I went to six football games last fall because they were "big games." Now it was basketball season, and a new round of "big games" was about to start. Gag.

"Friday night is movie night at Ashleigh's," I said. It wasn't, but it would be. I just had to talk to Ashleigh about it.

"But it's the biggest game of the year," Kellie whined. "You'll miss my back handspring."

I'd seen Kellie's back handspring. And her round-off. I'd also seen her back layout with half twist and every jump and split known to man. I had a pretty good feeling I knew what it looked like. Besides, after a while, all that showing off made it look like someone flopping across the gym floor to me.

"Sorry," I said with a shrug. "I have a life too, you know."

It was kind of a rude thing to say, but it felt really good.

A surge of adrenaline actually shot through my body when I said it. It was about time I tried to point that out to everyone because, even now, I would swear my parents think my world revolves around Kellie like theirs does.

"Mia!" Mom scolded. I'm not sure why she was whispering, since Kellie was sitting closer to her than I was. But the good news was, while my brain was working overtime trying to come up with a way to get out of this without apologizing, the car slowed to a stop and I realized we were in front of my school.

"What's with that box?" Kellie asked. "Some supersecret spy stuff?"

I could tell she was being sarcastic, but I guess I deserved it after what I'd just said. "Valentine's Day stuff."

"For the roses," Mom added. "Mia's selling chocolate roses for Valentine's Day."

Kellie perked right up. "I did that once," she said. "Ours were carnations in different colors."

"White for friendship, red for love?" Mom asked. "We did that when I was in school."

"What was yellow?" Kellie asked Mom. "I thought yellow was friendship."

While they hashed that out, I opened the box and looked

inside. Stacks of cards, all ready to be filled out. We just had to sell them.

"Mia's going to win a lock-in," Mom announced.

I hadn't been listening to the conversation, so I wasn't sure how that had come up. I just kept going through my cards, making sure they were all stacked evenly.

"You mean one of those things where you spend the night in your school gym?" Kellie asked.

"This one will be at the Sportsplex," I replied, feeling a little defensive. "There's ice skating and pizza and all kinds of other stuff."

The lock-in would be fun, but if anyone thought that was why I was fighting to sell more roses . . . wrong, wrong, *wrong*. Winning the lock-in would show everyone I could do something. I'd be something besides invisible for a change. I really, really wanted that.

"And Mia's going to win," Mom said.

"It runs in the family," Kellie said. "Our seventh-grade class won a big pizza party–movie day when I was in charge of sales. It's so easy to do. Tell the guys with girlfriends if they don't buy flowers for them, their girlfriends will be mad."

I frowned. I didn't know very many guys with girl-friends. Even if I did, that wouldn't work. Even in seventh grade, Kellie had been drop-dead gorgeous. All she had to do was walk up to a boy and he'd buy all the flowers she had.

"I'll have to give that a try," I said. "Thanks."

"Get your friends to buy roses for you," Kellie said, spinning around to look at me. "I got five roses in each color. That made us *so* much money. It works. Try it."

I stared at her for a long moment. As annoying as Kellie's perfectness was, she was a supergood sister. How could I ever be mad at her? Plus, she seemed to have no idea that I was a total loser compared to her. She always seemed to think I should be able to do whatever she did. It was annoying—and it made me feel bad for being annoyed.

Thankfully, Mom had pulled up in front of the school by then. The good news was, Mom actually had been listening when I asked to be dropped off first.

"Gotta go," I said, reaching for the door handle and jumping out, balancing the box under one arm as I closed the door. I took off for the school so fast my backpack bounced against my back in an almost painful way.

CHAPTER TWO

♥

To: Ashleigh
From: Mia
Let's sell some roses!

I slowed down as I made my way through the front door of school, but I still walked quickly, making a beeline for the cafeteria. Our table was directly facing the eighth-grade table, so we could see they weren't selling many either. Each grade sold only to their own grade. The class that sold the most roses won.

"Hey, hey, hey," Ashleigh said as I dropped down next to her. Besides possibly winning the day for my grade, the only good thing about all this rose-selling stuff was being able to do it with my BFF. Everyone in seventh grade was excited that we'd win a lock-in if we sold more roses than the other grades. If we won, I'd be the talk of the school.

Ashleigh, being the BFF she was, had agreed to suffer with me to help me out. She didn't really get my obsession with winning, but I was grateful she was there.

"Hey." My voice had much less enthusiasm than hers.

"What did Kellie do this time?" Ashleigh asked immediately.

"Kellie has a big game Friday night," I said, deciding to skip over the part where she told me how great she was at selling flowers. Ashleigh and I shared a look. That was the awesome thing about a BFF who had been your BFF for, like, *ever*. You knew each other's histories. You got things without having to spend an hour and a half explaining them. It saved a lot of time.

"Let me guess," Ashleigh said. "She's being crowned best cheerleader ever in the history of cheerleading."

"She learned new ways to show off," I said, shrugging. "So you're having movie night."

Ashleigh looked over at me, her eyes widening by the second. "I am?" Then, after thinking about it a second, she nodded. "Oh. So you can get out of going to the game."

"Exactly."

"Exactly what?"

That was Alex's voice, coming from behind us. Alex was

my BMFF (best *male* friend forever). He was the only one who'd go to the trouble of finding us before school.

"Looky who showed up to help," Ashleigh said, knowing full well he had no intention of helping. He thought all this stuff was silly.

Or at least he pretended he did.

I tilted my head to the side a little and eyed Alex suspiciously. He'd changed recently, and I couldn't put my finger on how. He used to hang out with us all the time, cutting up and punching me in the arm every time he got the chance. Now he was always acting all "cool," like he was suddenly better than us.

Alex picked up my notepad and started reading the names on it.

"Hey." I reached up and snatched the notepad out of his hand. "No peeking. Those are top secret."

He grabbed a chair and scooted it over before plopping down on it. He was sitting in the chair backward for some reason, but I knew if I asked him why, he'd just shrug and say one word: *Because.*

"Did you hang the sign?" I asked Ashleigh. We had another fifteen minutes before class. If she hadn't hung the sign near the seventh-grade lockers, I'd have to do something super soon. The three of us were sitting at a table in the huge cafeteria all alone.

"Yes," Ashleigh said. "Maybe I should send myself a rose."

She picked up the foil-covered chocolate rose we'd set out as a sample. It looked just like a real rose, with a green stem and red foil at the top. Only beneath that red foil was chocolate.

"It sucks to sit there, watching everyone else get roses," she added.

I watched Ashleigh's face. She looked like she didn't care, but I knew she did. We all did. And that was why this whole thing really stunk, possible lock-in or not. It would never be fun because it would never be fair.

"Warning, warning," Alex said softly. We both looked at him. He was staring straight ahead, where the girl I wanted to see less than anyone else in the whole universe was walking toward us. Kaylee Hooper.

I looked up to see her staring down at me. Tall and thin with a perfect nose and straight, even teeth, Kaylee was the seventh grader everyone wanted to be like. She even had a dimple on the right side of her mouth when she smiled, just like Jennifer Lawrence. I liked to think of her as Kellie 2.0.

Oh, and in case I forgot to mention it—right after I volunteered to sell roses, Kaylee reminded us, very loudly, that last year the sixth graders sold more chocolate roses in the history of chocolate roses themselves. We got a new computer in the computer lab *and* a pizza party, which was last year's prize. I never really thought all of that stuff could have come from selling one-dollar roses, but whatever. Maybe Kaylee put extra money in to pay for the computer and pizza party. She was head of the committee last year, so it would have made her look good.

Whatever happened last year, Kaylee's message was clear. If I messed this up, I'd be messing up something that was really, really good before I got my little hands on it.

"Hi," I said back, trying to remember the last time Kaylee had spoken to me. Sometime last year, as best I could remember, and even then I think the most she'd said to me was, "Excuse me," because I was in her way.

"I would like to purchase seven roses," Kaylee said, handing over a ten-dollar bill.

Seven roses. I held myself back from rolling my eyes. It didn't take a genius to figure out where those seven roses were going. Seven roses for her seven closest girlfriends, otherwise known as the seventh-grade cheerleading squad. They'd all get roses for each other, and Ashleigh and I would spend the morning handing them out to those same eight girls.

I held out the notepad and told her to write down the names and the message she wanted written on each card. She just stared at it.

"To Christina, to Faith, to Rosalia, to Claire, to Makayla, to Shonda, and to Ella," she recited. Then she stopped to stare at me. "Aren't you going to write this down?"

Sighing, I turned the notepad around and wrote *Kaylee's friends* on the next seven lines. I'd list out all the names after Kaylee was gone.

"Message?" I asked, looking up at her.

"From Kaylee," she said as though that should be obvious. She then rolled her eyes and stomped off.

"Wait!" Ashleigh called out. "You forgot your change." She looked at me, waving the ten-dollar bill around. "She forgot her change."

"Maybe it's our tip," I said. "Do you want to chase after her with it?"

Ashleigh thought about that a minute before putting it in the cashbox. No doubt she was picturing us walking up to Kaylee with three one-dollar bills, holding them out, and Kaylee looking at us like we were annoying her.

No, thank you.

I stared at the box in front of us, filled with blank cards. Two Valentine's Day committee volunteers would get together after school to fill all the cards out for our grade.

On my notepad were the names of the few people who had bought roses in the past week. I'd been counting on a bunch of people showing up today. That wasn't happening. If I didn't figure something out, we'd lose this contest, and I'd go down in history forever as the girl who ruined the Valentine's Day fund-raiser.

I imagined the look on my parents' faces when they realized I wasn't as good as Kellie . . . and never would be. Maybe I'd even lose my seat in the back squished next to Kellie's projects, and have to walk to school. Probably not. My parents always said they were proud of me no matter what I did. But I knew parents were supposed to say things like that.

As I looked at the blank cards in the box, I suddenly realized how easy it would be to put names on each of those cards and attach them to roses tonight. I could afford it if I used some of the babysitting money I'd been saving for a new phone. I could slip it into the cashbox before I turned it in tomorrow morning. It would be worth every dime.

I rolled my pen between my thumb and forefinger,

staring down at the notepad in front of me. We'd write the cards based on what was on that notepad. What if, after Alex and Ashleigh rushed off to class, I said that I'd sold a few more roses? With so many people filling out cards, chances were nobody would notice the big chunk of names and messages at the end.

I could write whatever I wanted and nobody would know the difference. And I didn't have to send them all to "Kaylee's friends," either. I could play Cupid and make sure that this year, Cupid's arrow didn't strike just the popular people. They'd be happy and I'd win the contest, showing that I could do something as well as Kellie and Kaylee for a change.

I smiled to myself. This year was going to be the best Valentine's Day ever.

CHAPTER THREE

❤

To: Ashleigh

From: Mia

I hope you don't figure out I sent all these roses.

The next morning, I took a deep breath and stared down at the stack of roses on the rolling cart in the school office. I had a good reason to be so nervous. Before yesterday's meeting, I'd snuck into the girls' restroom to write twenty-five messages at the bottom of the list. Each message had been from a "secret admirer," and those names had ended up on twenty-five cards. I'd checked to make sure they were all there while we were loading up the cart before school. I didn't even want to think about the trouble I'd be in if I got caught. Could I get in serious trouble? Would I even be in trouble, since I'd paid for them out of my own pocket?

I just had to forget about that and hand them out.

The bell rang, signaling the beginning of homeroom. Time to roll.

My heart pounded as I opened the door and Ashleigh pushed the cart through. She had no idea one of those roses was for her. I'd made sure hers was on the bottom.

Homerooms at Stanton Middle School were organized by last names alphabetically, making this a piece of cake. We'd organized the roses by last name. We headed toward the classroom where the *A*s through *C*s were and knocked.

"I think Cupid's here," the always-cheerful Ms. Michaletz said as she whipped the door open and waved us in. Both Ashleigh and I were wearing red, knowing everyone would be watching us.

Two of Kaylee's girls and four people receiving fake secret admirer roses, including Gillianni Carter, were in this homeroom. Gillianni was pretty, but she hid behind long, straight hair and baggy clothes. She had this *I don't care* look about her that tended to scare people off. But she didn't scare me.

I gave Faith and Shonda theirs first, taking in their smug smiles before looking over at Gillianni. She seemed to almost shrink into the background as she stared sadly down at her notebook. I knew if anyone asked her, she'd say she didn't want a rose, but we all wanted roses. Nobody wanted to sit back and watch everyone else get attention. I knew the feeling.

We handed out six more roses—mostly from girls to boys they were going out with—until all that was left were the four secret admirer roses. I handed two to Ashleigh, and I took the other two, including Gillianni's.

First there was a rose for Sun Patterson, a girl everyone called "Bucktooth" behind her back because of her long front teeth. As I walked slowly toward her, the two roses clutched tightly in front of me, she watched with a hopeful look on her face. I clearly remembered sitting across from her last year, when she had that same hopeful expression. That expression had fallen when one of Kaylee's friends had smugly continued on past to give the rose to someone else. Not this year.

This year I stopped in front of her and, with a huge smile on my face, handed one of the chocolate roses to her. I'd written something about her pretty eyes—light blue with long, perfect eyelashes—on the notepad. Those eyes almost seemed to twinkle as she took the rose and set it down on her desk. She was probably waiting until later to open the card, when people weren't staring at her.

Now for Gillianni. I didn't know her all that well, but I'd never forgotten the time she'd stood up for me. It was second grade and we were at a school roller-skating party. Three of the girls, including Kaylee's "girl" Christina, had tripped me, then stood over me laughing. Gillianni skated over and faced off with them, telling them to stop being such jerks.

As I walked toward her, she still didn't lift her head. She was staring down at an open notebook on her desk, probably studying or something. Either she was convinced I was going to someone else or she didn't want to get her hopes up. I kept my gaze on her as I approached, rose held out in front of me.

Even when I was standing in front of her, she didn't look up. I had no other choice. I set the rose down on the desk in front of her and stepped back. No way was I walking off before I saw her reaction.

Slowly she moved her head until she could see the rose. She stared at it, her expression blank. I waited for her to reach out and take it, but finally I had no choice. I had to go.

"Mia," Ashleigh whispered. Everyone turned to look at me.

I backed away from Gillianni, who had returned her attention to her notebook again. She'd look at the card on her chocolate rose as soon as she thought nobody was watching her. She'd look at it and smile for the first time probably *ever*. That was what I told myself, anyway.

I turned and headed back toward Ashleigh. She was already rolling the cart toward the door, the stack of roses looking as high as it had been when we walked in here.

The next class was stocked with Kaylee's friends. Including Kaylee, there were six of them. It wasn't so hard to hand roses to them now that I knew other people were getting them too. Like Alex, who was seated at the very back of the room.

Part of me wanted to give Alex his rose first, but I knew him. He didn't care if he got a rose or not. What Alex was doing was watching me with a big smirk on his face. He was laughing deep down inside because I had to do this. I'd make a face at him, but everyone was watching.

Kaylee got twelve roses. Seven were from her friends, two were from boys she'd probably never even noticed, two were from girls who were kissing up to her in hopes of becoming her friends, and one wasn't signed. Ashleigh took care of handing those over while I handled the rest of her friends. There was nothing fun about giving roses to that group. They fully expected it. But the other people, like the girls who got flowers from their boyfriends, were more than worth it. Their eyes lit up, and they looked like they wanted to jump up and down.

Because Ashleigh finished first, she was the one who handed Alex's rose to him. I turned around and there she was, standing in front of him. He stared at the rose like it was some kind of foreign object and finally reached out and took it. As Ashleigh made her way back to me, I found myself frowning at her. Alex was her friend too, so I guess it was selfish for me to want to be the one to hand it to him. There was no way she could know I was the one who sent it.

I glanced back at him as we rolled out of the room. He was reading the writing on the card attached to the rose. I had to fight back a smile as I remembered what I'd written.

Once I was in the hallway, I paused for a second to think about what I was doing. There was a good chance this was going to work. I mentally patted myself on the back. If I pulled this off, that meant I could finally win something like Kellie always did. If our grade could win the lock-in, I'd be a hero, for sure. And I was boosting everyone in the process!

We barely had time to hand out the rest of the roses before the final bell rang. As we walked out of the last homeroom, I was still holding Ashleigh's rose. I'd grabbed it off the cart to make sure she didn't see it until I was ready.

We were in the hallway, surrounded by people rushing around us, when finally she turned to look at me. That was when she saw the rose I was holding.

"You forgot one?" she asked. She looked at the classroom door we'd just exited, as if judging whether or not we could go back at this point.

"It's yours," I said, holding it out to her.

Of all the roses I'd given out, that was the one that was the most exciting. Just to see her changing expressions—from boredom to confusion to hope to excitement—was worth all the trouble I'd gone through writing all those names and messages. This was definitely the best idea I'd ever had.

"You mean it's for me?" she asked, still not reaching for it.

I thrust it toward her. "Take it. I'll get this cart back to the office."

I couldn't bring myself to stand there while she read the card. I guess I felt like she'd figure out I'd written it if I was standing there.

"Wait."

I was several banks of lockers away when I heard Ashleigh calling for me. She was rushing to catch up.

"Who wrote this?" she asked.

"What do you mean?" I played totally dumb. Maybe that

wasn't a good idea. It had only been a few seconds since we were talking about the rose, after all.

"Who sent this rose to me?" she asked. "And these words. They're beautiful. Who bought this rose for me?"

My footsteps faltered a little, but I kept rolling the cart. "I don't know," I said quickly.

"You have to know," she said.

This time I looked over at her. I nearly ran over someone before quickly straightening the cart again. She knew. I should have known she'd know. We were BFFs. BFFs knew each other's cheesy writing.

"All the seventh-grade cards were sold by either you or me," Ashleigh said. "It wasn't me, so the person had to have bought the flower from you."

Oh. Great. That was something that hadn't occurred to me. I'd been so stressed about getting the flowers sold, I'd totally spaced on this part of it.

"It was on the cart," I said. "I don't know where it came from."

Not the best cover story, but I didn't have much time. Plus, I wasn't very good at lying.

Ashleigh thought about that a minute before speaking.

"He must have bought it from one of the other grades. I guess anyone who liked me would know we're friends, so that makes sense. I mean, the guy couldn't walk up to you and tell you he was my secret admirer, could he?"

I shook my head, but she wasn't looking at me anyway. She was looking all around her. I knew Ashleigh. At this very minute, every guy who walked by was being closely looked at with the question, *Is that my secret admirer?*

"Go on to class," I said. "I'll drop the cart off."

It might make me late for class, but at least it would get me away from this conversation. Ashleigh was all glassy-eyed by then, so she didn't seem to even hear me. I rushed for the office before she could call out to me again.

"Hartley."

The sound of my last name made me freeze. No one called me that. I turned around to see four girls from the soccer team heading straight toward me. They were headed up by Trudie Kepler, the best athlete at our school, who some girls had made fun of until she got bigger than them.

I was a little scared of Trudie myself. I'd thought that by giving her one of the twenty-five secret admirer roses, I might get her to soften up a little. Plus, I'd never seen Trudie Kepler smile. I thought giving her a rose would maybe take away that mean look she always had on her face. I'd been wrong.

"Who sent this?" she asked.

She stopped in front of me, a hand one hip, the rose in her other hand. Her friends were lined up on either side of her. This wasn't looking good.

I looked down at her rose. The attached note had referred to her soft side, and I'd been hoping it might bring it out. At the moment, it didn't look likely.

"I don't know," I said.

"You have to know." She held up the card, which she'd detached from the rose at some point. "You're the one who sold it to the person."

"Some of the roses weren't bought before school," I said. That was a good cover story, even though it wasn't true. I decided I'd use that with anyone else who asked. "I don't know where they came from."

I hated lying, but I didn't have a choice at this point. I just told myself I was doing this to help others, so it was worth it.

Trudie's hard-as-steel expression loosened up a little. She stepped back, her shoulders falling, and looked far less like she was about to punch me. I suddenly realized I'd been holding my breath this whole time and let it out.

"How will I find out who sent it?" Trudie asked, looking down at the rose. "I need to know."

That was another question I hadn't prepared to answer. I thought for a second. It was important to come up with a good answer for this question.

"How was it signed?" I asked.

"Secret admirer," one of Trudie's friends piped up to say. "She has a secret admirer? What does that even mean?"

"It means someone admires her but in secret," one of Trudie's other friends said.

"Hush," Trudie said. She turned her beady eyes back on me. "You're telling me someone filled out one of your cards without you knowing?"

"Sixth and eighth graders were selling roses," I said, shrugging. "Maybe your crush isn't in this grade."

That was the same cover story I'd used with Ashleigh. I wasn't sure if it had worked on her, but it was worth a try on other people. Trudie looked like she was about to say something else, but the warning bell rang, reminding us all we were going to be late for first period.

"I have to go," I said, stepping backward as I pushed the

cart forward behind me. "Congratulations on the whole rose thing. Not everyone got one."

I held out my left hand to show it was empty. Then I looked up. There, on the faces of a couple of Trudie's friends, was a look I knew all too well. It was that same sad look I'd seen on flowerless people's faces last year. Pity.

No roses for me. I suddenly felt really, really sad about that. Maybe I should have sent myself one, just to fit in.

As I turned and rolled the cart back toward the office, I looked around. Roses everywhere. I didn't know which was sadder—not having a rose or the fact that the only way I could have gotten a rose was if I'd sent it to myself. So much for feeling less invisible. Suddenly I felt more invisible than ever.

CHAPTER FOUR

♥

To: Alex

From: Mia

I miss the days when we could just hang out without all this weird stuff between us.

After a morning of watching everyone show off their roses, I headed into the cafeteria to sit at a table full of people showing off their roses. I was actually a little bummed. My brilliant plan was turning out to be not the best plan ever for me. I had to listen to everyone talk about their roses while I had nothing.

"You ate yours?" Ashleigh was asking Alex. "Seriously?"

Alex shrugged. "What was I supposed to do? It's chocolate."

"Save it." She looked over at me and rolled her eyes before turning back to him. "Tell me you at least still have the stem."

"Why would I save that?" He bit into his sandwich and looked at me while he chewed. Like I had an answer for that.

"Sentimental value," Ashleigh said. "Boys are so blah." She looked at me. "Did you hear Sun Patterson got a rose?"

One of Ashleigh's science classmates stuck her teeth over her lower lip and began imitating a squirrel. Ashleigh didn't laugh, but the other girls down at that end of the table did. All I could think was how glad I was that I'd given Sun a rose. It would suck for someone to be making fun of me like that.

Sadness washed over me again as I remembered that look of pity Trudie's friends had given me just that morning. Wasn't this the same thing? People could be making fun of me, too, for all I knew. After all, at least Sun had gotten a rose.

"Sun's pretty cool," Alex said. "She's in my sixth period."

"She *is* kind of cool." I looked at Ashleigh. "You should get to know her."

Instead of looking ashamed of herself, as she should have, she gave me her *what's up with you?* look. "Playing Cupid turned you into a weirdo," she said. Then she looked at Alex. "And you've always been one."

Alex shrugged off her statement and continued eating his sandwich. I, meanwhile, had an agenda of my own.

"So," I said, leaning forward to put myself closer to Alex. "Who sent you the rose?"

Alex dragged his gaze—reluctantly—from his sandwich and narrowed his eyes at me. "You know who sent it," he said.

My heart did a little jump-skip. He was onto me. I leaned back in my chair, shaking my head. But denying it would be a waste of energy. Nobody knew me as well as Alex. Except maybe Ashleigh, and she was off in her own world right now.

"I do not," I said.

Hey, I had to try, right?

"Do too," he said.

"Why would I know who sent you a chocolate rose? That makes no sense," I argued.

"You were the person who sold it," he said. "I'd know your handwriting anywhere."

I looked at Ashleigh, who now was eyeing me with interest. "I didn't write any of the cards," I said. At least that much was true. I looked at Ashleigh. "Tell him."

"The committee just wrote what was on the sheet," Ashleigh said. "Mia and I took almost all the orders for seventh grade."

All of them, actually. But I'd keep that part to myself.

Alex looked back at me. "So you know who paid for the

rose because you're the one who took the order. Spill it."

They were both staring at me. Oh, the pressure. That was when I remembered what I'd told Trudie.

"Other grades were taking money too," I said. "If someone in sixth grade bought a rose for you, a sixth grader would have filled out the card. I also got some last-minute orders and they were all rushed. I didn't know what those said. You could have been one of those."

"You had last-minute orders?" Ashleigh asked. "I didn't see that."

"It was yesterday morning," I said with a shrug. I didn't like to lie, but I had no other choice. "You and Alex left for class early."

"It could have been an eighth grader," Alex said.

I looked over at him and realized he was more focused on who sent the rose than on what I was saying. I nodded. It could have been an eighth grader. An eighth grader *could* have a crush on Alex. Why not? He was cute for a boy, I guessed. Kind of geeky with his obsession with movies, but cute for *someone*, I was sure.

"What?" Alex asked. He gave me a strange look. I didn't like that look. I didn't know what it meant, but it made me feel all squirmy.

I realized that I was staring at him and jerked my gaze away. "Nothing," I said.

"Where's the list?" Ashleigh asked, obviously not even noticing the weird thing going on right in front of her. "Maybe we can recognize the handwriting."

Alex perked up at that. "I'd like to see it," he said. "Where is it?"

Uh-oh. "I . . . uh . . . threw it away," I said quickly. The office had a copy of all the lists, so I was hoping they wouldn't check.

They seemed to buy that. Thank goodness. I certainly didn't want to spend the evening faking different handwriting on a pretend list to show them.

"It's weird," Ashleigh said, lowering her voice to barely above a whisper. "Knowing someone has a crush on you. I keep looking around, and every time I catch someone looking at me, I wonder if that's *him*."

I held back a smile. That made it totally worth it. Ashleigh was happier than I'd seen her in months. I'd given her something to look forward to and somebody to focus on besides Rob Martocci, the guy she'd been crushing on since forever.

"Do you think it's Rob?" Alex asked.

I gave him a look. Was he for real? I'd finally gotten her

to think about something besides Rob for once, and he was actually bringing it up. I realized maybe that wouldn't help her get over him if she thought he sent it.

Luckily, the bell rang, ending the conversation before it could get worse. I hopped up and headed toward the tray return without waiting for either of them to catch up with me. If I could avoid talking about crushes and Cupid and Valentine's Day stuff the rest of the day, that would be perfect.

Unfortunately, my parents had other plans. Every year for Valentine's Day, my parents give my sister and me flowers and heart-shaped boxes of candy. Which meant that every year, it was the *only* thing I got for Valentine's Day. While all my friends received chocolate roses from people they thought were secret admirers, I came home empty-handed. So much for karma. I knew it shouldn't bother me. After all, I was the one who wrote all those cards.

But it kind of did.

My mom totally geeked out when it came to Valentine's Day—or any holiday, for that matter. You should see what she did on Halloween. For Valentine's Day this year, she ordered one of those heart-shaped pizzas and surrounded it with pink-frosted cupcakes.

"Surprise!" she yelled when Dad walked through the door. He looked genuinely surprised, probably because of the crazy number of candles Mom had lit all over the room. A strong breeze would set this whole place on fire.

"Well, well," he said. "What's this all about?"

"Can we eat now?" Kellie asked, staring down at her phone. She would rather be anywhere than hanging out with our parents on Valentine's Day, but they had a strict "home on school nights" rule that they wouldn't let her break no matter how many times she complained, *But that's not fair!* It was the only time they didn't give in to her demands.

When finally we were all seated—I was starting to worry the pizza would get cold—we had to deal with one difficult question. "How was your Valentine's Day?" Dad asked all of us.

Dad meant well. He probably thought he was merely making small talk. But a question that on any other day would bring up bored responses of "Fine" from both of us and be okay was a much bigger question on Valentine's Day.

"Fine," I said. Because I didn't really want to go into it. I hoped he'd leave it at that.

"Oh, you can do better than that," Dad said. "Did Cupid's arrow strike?"

He asked the question with a big gleam in his eye. I knew he didn't actually think Cupid's arrow struck anything. This was Dad, the guy who had told us we couldn't start dating until we were thirty-eight. I was starting to think he might get his wish. With me, anyway.

Of course, he didn't ask a question like that to Kellie. He didn't have to ask. Kellie had a boyfriend, as we all knew, and that boyfriend had sent her two dozen roses at school. Because one dozen just wasn't enough, I guess.

"Yes," I said. "The cutest boy in school chased me around all morning."

Dad's eyes widened, and his mouth stopped moving mid-chew. "Don't be sarcastic, Mia," Mom chimed in to say. "And Kellie, sit up straight."

Dad started chewing again, his expression changing to relief. What? Was it that hard to believe that a boy might actually like me? Wait. I hadn't said *a* boy liked me. I'd said the cutest boy in school liked me. Maybe that was pushing it too far. But still!

"Did he catch you?" Kellie asked.

I'd been picking the sausage off my pizza, but Kellie's question caused me to look up from that engrossing activity. "What?" I asked.

"The cutest boy in school," she continued around a mouthful of food. "You said he'd been chasing you around all day. Did he catch you?"

Kellie gave me a look that dared me to answer the question. She wanted to embarrass me. She wanted to point out in her own little way that I could never, ever have a boyfriend.

"She was joking, Kellie," Dad said. In his eyes, Kellie would never do anything mean. She was his perfect angel.

"How do you know that?" I asked Dad. "Do you just assume no boy would like me?"

"Mia Hartley, don't be so dramatic," Mom said. "And quit picking at your food."

"I'm not that bad," I said. "Boys like me."

Except the lack of a rose totally said otherwise. But I really wasn't a freak or anything. I wasn't the most beautiful girl in school, but I was okay. Boys just didn't pay attention to girls unless you were Kaylee or one of her friends, and they only liked guys who went to other schools.

"Nobody said you were that bad." Mom sighed and

looked at Dad. "Grant, explain what I'm trying to say."

"You're young," Dad said. "You have plenty of time to worry about boys. Focus on your schoolwork."

Why did that sound so familiar? Oh yeah, because they said those same words to me and Kellie every sixteen days or so. Whatever. I had a feeling that when they were my age they were worried about the same things I was worried about.

"Can I go?" Kellie asked, pushing away from the table.

"You hardly ate anything," Mom said, staring at her empty plate, which had held a slice of pizza a few minutes ago.

"I had a slice," Kellie said, already standing, cell phone in hand.

"Oh," Mom said. "I thought we could have family time." She looked disappointed.

"Mm-hmm." Kellie was distracted. She stood and started slowly walking toward her bedroom. Even though Mom was upset, she wouldn't stop her.

"So," Dad said, lifting his gaze from his plate to me. "What's going on at school?"

I would have rolled my eyes and stomped off to my room, just to see if I could get away with it. But I was hungry and the pizza was really good. Besides, they wouldn't let me get away with it anyway, I was pretty sure.

"Mia handed out roses for Valentine's Day," Mom announced. She reached for another slice. "Tell your father about that, Mia."

"No big deal," I said with a shrug. "People bought roses. I handed them out."

"Why?" Dad asked.

I stopped chewing to stare at him. *Why?* What did that mean?

Noticing my confused look, he added, "Was it for charity or something?"

I'd almost forgotten about the reason we'd been handing out roses in the first place. I'd cheated and paid for a bunch of the roses out of my babysitting money—all just to win the contest.

"The winning grade gets a lock-in," I said. "But we probably won't win. We didn't sell very many."

That was true, if you subtracted the twenty-five I bought from the total. I'd rather have a sleepover with my friends than a lock-in with the whole grade, but I wanted to win. I just had to listen to everyone talk about their roses to get to the big announcement that our grade had won.

"Didn't Kellie do that when she was in middle school?" Dad asked Mom.

"Hers were carnations," Mom said. "Remember when she brought all those flowers home?"

Dad nodded. "Don't remind me! She had plenty of admirers."

"I'm sure she still does," Mom says. "They just know she has a boyfriend now."

Okay, I'd officially lost my appetite. Even when they asked about me, it always managed to go back to Kellie. The last thing I wanted to do was sit here and listen to how great Kellie was and how everyone liked her. Maybe this Cupid thing wasn't working like I thought it would.

CHAPTER FIVE

♥

To: Sun

From: Mia

What have I gotten myself into?

"Whoa."

Alex and I were standing in the hallway before home-room, waiting for Ashleigh to get her books out of her locker. I'd been watching everyone who walked by, searching for someone who'd gotten a rose yesterday. I was wondering if anyone would suddenly "couple up" as a result of the secret admirer roses.

"What?" I asked, turning to look at Alex. To be honest, I'd forgotten he was standing next to me.

He didn't answer. He didn't have to. I followed his stare to Sun Patterson, who was breezing past. I couldn't believe what I was seeing.

She was still wearing her baggy clothes and her hair still had a bad case of the frizzies. But she was standing up straight and looking around. She seemed to have a glow that made her stand out.

"She looks . . . great," Alex said, causing me to whip my head around to stare at him. He looked at me. "What? She does."

Shaking my head, I watched her as she passed us and disappeared into the crowd. I assumed this new confidence had something to do with the rose she'd gotten yesterday. It had to, right?

Sun thought someone had a crush on her, so she was feeling prettier. Maybe it had even given her a crazy big rush of confidence. None of that could be bad. I'd helped her, and now someone would have a crush on her and it would be okay that there wasn't a real secret admirer.

"What are we looking at?"

Ashleigh had stepped into place next to me and was staring down the hall at the mass of people. No sign of Sun at all.

"Sun Patterson," I said. "Alex is having a meltdown because she looks so good."

Ashleigh squinted at me. She wasn't buying that at all, I could tell. She'd see soon enough.

"Gotta go," Alex said, stepping away from us. "See you in second period?"

I nodded and followed Ashleigh toward class. "You should have seen her. I think getting that rose gave her confidence."

I said the last part on purpose, because even though she hadn't seen Sun yet, I was wondering what she thought about the whole rose thing.

"Who?" Ashleigh asked.

"Sun," I said, giving her a sideways look. Was she even listening to me?

"Oh. I'd have to see her."

My gaze landed on something then. I grabbed Ashleigh's arm and nodded toward Kurt Barnes.

"What?" she asked. She was looking right at him too.

"Kurt Barnes," I said. "You don't see it?"

"I see *him*," she said. "What about him?"

"He's walking straighter."

Kurt was passing us by then, and he noticed we'd stopped to stare at him. He gave us an odd look, probably wondering what was going on. But he nervously snapped his gaze toward the area in front of him again.

"Whatever," Ashleigh said. "I think you're looking for things."

"He has more confidence, I know he does," I said, but I was pretty much talking to myself at that point. People were beginning to scurry toward homeroom, so she became focused on getting to class on time.

But I kept thinking about Kurt, even after I sat down in homeroom and waited for class to start. Kurt was different. I could tell. Getting a rose had made him feel better about himself. Sure, he still wore the same plain T-shirt and way-out-of-style jeans, but just that one little difference made him cuter somehow.

It was worth it. Even if I didn't get one . . . of course it had been worth it.

"Question."

I blinked in surprise. Kaylee was standing in front of me, acting like she wanted to ask me a question. What question, though?

"Who sent the extra rose?"

Kaylee had received four extra roses on Valentine's Day. Two were from girls kissing up to her and two were from boys. I had no idea which of those she considered "extra."

"You know everyone who sent roses, right?" she asked. "There was one that wasn't signed. Who sent it?"

I honestly had no idea. Maybe I should have, but the whole rose thing had been such a blur of activity, there was no way to know for sure. Ashleigh had probably taken that one down. I was pretty sure I'd remember a boy sending a rose to Kaylee and refusing to sign his name to it.

"I don't know," I said, knowing she probably wouldn't believe that at all.

She didn't. "Come on," she said. "You have to tell me. I'd tell you. Was he at least someone cute?"

"I—" Now I was stuttering. I figured she'd laugh at me.

"Royal Jessup," she guessed. "Zachary Eggert. Bobby Featherstone."

The names weren't too random. All of them were semi-cute boys. Boys who at least kind of hung out in her wider circle of friends.

"I told you, I don't know," I said. "I don't remember any boy buying a rose for you and not signing his name to it."

Finally she seemed to be starting to believe me. "Could I maybe see the list?" she asked. "I might recognize the handwriting."

"I don't have my list, but you can check with Ashleigh. Whoever it was probably bought the rose from her." That was the truth—I really had no clue who it could be from.

Silence spread between us as Kaylee stared at me. It was hard not to think nice thoughts when you looked at her, she was so pretty, but she was also so stuck on herself, you realized she wasn't as pretty as she thought she was.

"I'll do that," Kaylee said. "I'll talk to her. Thanks."

She spun around, flouncing off down the hallway.

"What did she want?" Ashleigh asked. She'd come from out of nowhere.

"She wanted to know who her secret admirer was," I said. I shrugged. "I didn't do that rose. Did you?"

"Yep," Ashleigh said. "But she'll just have to wonder about her secret admirer like everyone else."

Everyone but me, I wanted to say.

"So?" I asked.

She'd been looking at a group of guys as they passed. My question snapped her head back around.

"So?" she asked in reply.

I sighed. "So who sent the rose?" I paused before adding, "To Kaylee."

"Oh, that." She waved her hand dismissively. "It's nothing."

I opened my mouth to argue, but before I could say anything, she spotted a girl from one of her classes and rushed off to ask her about homework. So much for that.

Sighing, I turned to walk toward class and nearly ran straight into Alex. He skidded to a halt, staring back at me with this strange, wide-eyed expression.

Why was Alex looking at me like that?

He'd been so weird lately. For a second, before he looked away, words flew through my mind that matched what I was seeing from him. He was looking at me like he'd never really seen me before.

"Sorry," he said.

I just stared at him, not blinking. I didn't like this new Alex at all. I wanted things back to the way they'd been before . . . before whenever he'd started acting so weird around me. I couldn't remember the exact date things had changed, but I didn't think anything had changed on my side. I was the same Mia Hartley I'd always been. Alex was the one who was acting all weird all of a sudden.

"Where are you going in such a hurry?" I asked, pasting a big smile on my face. I saw on TV once that if things are weird and you want them to get back to normal, you had to "fake it until you make it." So that was exactly what I did.

"Class," he said. He stepped back a little. "Where else?"

"I don't know," I said. I looked around. The halls were mostly empty, which meant the bell would ring any second now. We had to go.

I gave him one last look before spinning and rushing toward class. That look on his face stayed with me, though. Why was he acting so weird? And how could I get Alex back?

CHAPTER SIX

♥

To: Alex
From: Mia
Sun Patterson? Seriously?

I had just sat down at the lunch table when Ashleigh broke
the news.

"Alex likes Sun."

I stared at her a second before I realized what this was all
about. "Oh, that," I said. I slid my napkin from under my fork
and set it off to the side. "He just was surprised how different
she looked."

"No, he likes her," Ashleigh said. "He just told me."

"He *likes* likes her?" I asked. "But . . . why?"

"Shh, here he comes," Ashleigh said. "Are you going to
eat your apples?"

"Yes," I snapped. I didn't mean to be moody with Ashleigh,

but what was this about Alex liking someone? Anyone? He wasn't supposed to like girls. I didn't know why, but he wasn't.

As he plopped down next to me and acted like nothing at all had changed, I thought about that for a second. Everyone else in school had a crush on someone, so how fair was it to not allow him to? But of all people, *Sun Patterson*?

The only reason Sun Patterson was even the slightest bit appealing to Alex was that she'd gotten a rose and it had given her some confidence. She thought some boy, somewhere in this school, had a crush on her, and she was right. Now Alex had a crush on her and no telling who else.

"So I hear you like someone," I said.

Ashleigh gave me a harsh look. "Mia!"

"Alex tells me everything," I said. I looked over at him. "Why didn't you tell me?"

He was staring down at his lunch, and he looked really embarrassed. I felt bad for a second, but I felt even worse that he hadn't told me he liked someone.

"I told you this morning," he said.

"You said she looked great, but you didn't say you liked her," I pointed out.

"What's the difference?" Ashleigh asked.

"Lots of people are pretty," I said. "Liking someone is a

whole other thing. It means you think about that person all the time and . . . stuff."

I'm sure that sounded as fake to everyone else as it did to me. I looked down at my food to avoid seeing them staring at me like I was making no sense.

"You've never even thought a guy was cute," Ashleigh pointed out.

"Yes, I have," I said. Although I hadn't, really. But even if I had, I might not have told Ashleigh and Alex about it. They didn't have to know everything.

Ashleigh looked at Alex, a big smirk on her face. How annoying. I wanted to think someone was hot at that very minute, just to prove her wrong. I knew her next question would be, *Who?* and the truth was, I had no answer for that.

She opened her mouth. The question was coming and there was nothing I could do about it.

A shadow fell across her face, and she looked up. Her mouth stayed open, gaping, as she took in whatever was creating that shadow. Happy that something was interrupting her from asking that question, I spun around to see what she was looking at. Kaylee and crew were standing right behind me, glaring down at me.

I knew that look. They wanted answers, and they wanted them now.

"What's up?" Ashleigh asked casually. She'd always had more courage than I had. Or maybe it was just that she had no idea why they were standing there, looking all determined.

"We're here for answers," Kaylee said. Her hands were on her hips, her eyes narrowed as she glared at me. "And we're not leaving until we get them."

As if to prove her point, Kaylee and her group of friends sat. They scattered, sitting down on either side of me, Ashleigh, and Alex.

"Who sent the rose to Kaylee?" Claire asked.

"We want a name," Faith blurted.

"What are they talking about?" Ashleigh asked me.

I mirrored the annoyed look I saw on Ashleigh's face. Alex might be sitting there staring at Kaylee all goopy-eyed, but not me. I wasn't impressed by the little fashion model wannabe and her friends.

"Kaylee got an extra rose on Valentine's Day," I explained. As if Ashleigh didn't know. Ashleigh knew exactly who'd sent it.

"You're still on that?" Ashleigh asked. She rolled her eyes.

"What do you mean, I'm 'still on that'?" Kaylee asked.

"Of course I'm 'still on that.' I have a secret admirer out there somewhere. I want to know who it is."

"We don't know," Ashleigh said. She had to be lying, but it was her lie, not mine.

I couldn't help but wonder why she was lying, though. What was the big deal? If Ashleigh knew who had sent the chocolate rose—and she had already said she did—why didn't she just tell Kaylee?

"You have to know," Kaylee said. "Mia said you knew."

"Who do *you* think it is?" Alex asked. He still had this silly starstruck look in his eye, but at least he could talk to her.

Kaylee glanced over at him then. She gave him a look that seemed to make him shrink back in his chair.

"Was it you?" she asked.

The question was put harshly. Of course it wasn't him. Even if it had been, though, he wouldn't tell her. I knew him.

"It's a secret admirer," I said. I couldn't help it. I wanted to help him out. I wanted to save him. "That's what the word 'secret' means. It's supposed to be kept a secret."

Kaylee turned that stare on me now, but I refused to shrink back in my chair. I sat there, staring back at her without flinching.

"There are no secrets about me," Kaylee said. "I know everything."

Ashleigh snorted. I shared that feeling. This was silly, this whole thing. Why didn't Ashleigh just tell her who sent the rose and make her leave us alone?

"I want to see your lists," Kaylee said. She looked from me to Ashleigh and back again. "I want to look at every name until I find the person who bought my rose."

I looked at Ashleigh, who just rolled her eyes and picked up her sandwich and took a bite of it. Kaylee nodded to her friends, and all of them stood at once. They didn't even look back at us as they pranced back to their table in one big group.

"Just give her the list," Alex said. "She'll leave you alone."

"I don't have the list anymore," I said. And that wasn't a lie. I'd thrown it in the trash after the committee gave it back to me.

Ashleigh shrugged. "She can't order you around."

"No, but she can keep bugging us like this until we agree," I said. "I don't think any of us want that."

"I don't mind," Alex spoke up to say. When we all turned to look at him, he gave us a sheepish grin. "What? They're cute."

"You think everyone's cute," Ashleigh said.

That was exactly what I'd been thinking. "Not everyone," Alex said without looking at either of us.

"Not you," Ashleigh said.

My eyes widened. Not me? What kind of thing was that to say?

"Not me, either," Ashleigh said. "So don't feel bad."

Alex was suddenly very, very quiet. He didn't want anything to do with this conversation.

"You're frowning," Ashleigh said to me. "Do you like Alex or something?"

Silence. One of those long, awkward silences that made you wish you could just disappear out of sheer embarrassment. Even worse, Alex looked up as though he'd just snapped back to the present and realized what was going on.

"Does who like Alex?" Alex asked.

"Nobody," I said quickly, before Ashleigh could speak up. Maybe he hadn't heard. Maybe he couldn't piece two and two together and figure out I was the only person here she could have been asking, now that Kaylee and all her friends had taken off.

Then he looked at me. His eyes widened just barely. I probably wouldn't have noticed if I hadn't been looking at him so closely. I suddenly realized I was staring at him closely and quickly jerked my gaze away.

"I was just kidding around," Ashleigh said. "Come on. Time to go."

I hadn't realized it, but the cafeteria had started clearing out while I was staring down at my lunch. The bell must have rung and I hadn't even heard it. Whatever. I used the excuse to get out of there before Ashleigh could embarrass me further.

For the first time that I could remember, Alex didn't follow us.

CHAPTER SEVEN

♥

To: Kurt
From: Mia
Someone likes someone who likes you.

I didn't mean to walk out of school with Kurt Barnes. Really, I didn't. He was walking through the exit right ahead of me, and he held the door for me. It was totally random and surprised me, but what surprised me more was when Sun Patterson cornered me about it on the bus.

She actually got up from her seat and came back to sit next to me. This was after she'd gawked at me while I strolled past.

"Hey," she said.

I looked around, even though I knew there was no way she could be talking to someone else. She hadn't spoken to me since fourth grade, though, so it was weird she was suddenly sitting next to me like I was her longtime best friend or something.

"Hey," I said.

"I wanted to ask you something," she began.

I groaned, not even bothering to hold it in. I rolled my eyes, too. I knew exactly what this was about.

"I don't know who sent the rose," I said, exasperated. "There were a lot of people, and I was just trying to collect enough money for us to win the competition."

The whole "secret admirer" thing was something I'd done to be nice, but this was getting ridiculous. If I'd known everyone would be bugging me about it for the next few weeks, I might have thought about it a while longer.

"Huh?" Sun asked. She was looking at me like I was crazy or something. "No, I don't care about that. I wanted to ask you about Kurt Barnes."

Kurt Barnes. He'd gotten a rose too. Was she asking who sent *him* the rose? Because I didn't have an answer for that, either.

"Do you like him?" she asked.

That caught me off guard. I tried to figure out where she was coming from with that, but I couldn't. Maybe she'd noticed my handwriting on the card attached to his rose and thought I was his secret admirer or something.

"Why would I like him?" I asked. I wanted more information before I gave an answer.

"I saw you with him a few seconds ago," Sun said. "I thought you guys might be going out."

The weird thing about all this was the look on her face. She had this hopeful expression, like she was desperately clinging to everything I said.

She liked him. Wow. Sun Patterson liked Kurt Barnes.

"I've never even talked to him," I said. "But do *you* like him?"

I guess I expected Sun to deny it, but not even close. She looked down, a big, silly smile on her face.

The really strange thing about this conversation was I was relieved that she liked someone who wasn't Alex. Why was that? I didn't get it. Shouldn't I be happy that Alex might find someone he liked who liked him back?

"What are you doing about it?" I asked.

Her head snapped up. "What do you mean?" she asked.

"I mean, are you talking to him? Do you even know him?"

"I've never met him," she said. "I'm too shy."

"He might like you back, though," I said. "I don't know him, but I could introduce you if you'd like."

Her eyes lit up for a second. Then, seeming to realize something, she looked down again. "I don't think so. I'd just make a fool of myself."

So she was just going to keep liking him without talking to him . . . ever? What sense did that make?

I thought about it. That was what everyone did. They all seemed to get some crush on someone and never, ever talk to the person, going months and even years without getting to know the person they were thinking about all the time. It was an incredible waste of time. There had to be a better way.

They needed a matchmaker. And who better . . . than Cupid?

CHAPTER EIGHT

♥

To: Mia

From: Your Secret Admirer

You won't get away with it.

I stared at the words on the card in front of me, blinking several times to see if they'd change. They didn't, so I looked around to see if anyone was watching. Nobody was.

I got to school early to track down Kurt and talk to him about Sun. But when I'd opened my locker, a chocolate rose had fallen out. It was just like the ones we'd handed out on Valentine's Day, only it had a card attached—for *me*.

Somebody knew what I'd done and was trying to let me know everyone would eventually find out. But . . . who? My locker didn't have a lock on it, so it could have been anyone.

I looked around. Nobody was paying any attention to me, but that could be the trick. If the person who had put this rose in my locker was nearby, of course that person wouldn't want me to see someone was watching. I decided the best thing to do was shove the rose deep into my locker, cover it up with my coat, and close the door as quickly as possible. I'd figure it out later.

I slammed the door closed and rushed off down the hall. I was halfway to my class when I remembered my mission. Find Kurt and talk to him. I couldn't go to class until I did that.

I was still looking for Kurt when I saw something that stopped me in my tracks. *No.* It couldn't be.

Sure enough, it was. Gillianni was just a few feet away. Only her hair wasn't hanging down in her face and her head wasn't down. She was looking around with a paranoid expression, but she was *looking*. She usually never lifted her head and paid attention to what was around her.

Her gaze landed on me, catching me staring at her, and she quickly looked down and shuffled off. It was like she suddenly remembered she was supposed to not look at people.

"What's up with you?"

I'd know Alex's voice anywhere. He was, after all, my BMFF. Before things had gotten so weird between us, he'd sometimes call just to say hi. Now I was lucky if I got a text from him to ask some form of *What's up?*

"Nothing," I said. "I'm the same as I've always been."

He gave me a strange look. "Then why are you staring at Gillianni Carter?"

Oh. That was what he'd meant by, *What's up with you?* I'd thought he was talking about how we hardly talked anymore.

I could have said that. This was my chance. If we *were* BFFs, we should be able to talk about anything. But this weirdness between us was like a big brick wall.

"She looks . . . different," I said. "She wasn't staring down at the ground like she normally does."

My first thought was that now he'd decide he liked Gillianni instead of Sun Patterson. That bothered me too, and I didn't understand why.

"You're weird," he said.

That was it. That was how things had gotten between us. He never spoke more than he had to, and now, it felt like he always worked in some way to insult me. He either called me weird or strange or a dork.

It hurt my feelings, but I knew what he'd say if I told him that. He'd tell me to quit being a dork.

"Gotta go," he said. "See ya."

And that was it. That was probably the longest conversation we'd have all day. I sighed and started toward homeroom.

I couldn't worry about it now. I had too many other things going on.

I was halfway there before I remembered what my original goal had been. I was supposed to be playing matchmaker for Kurt and Sun. Did I have enough time?

I quickened my step and took off toward Kurt's homeroom. I'd just have to make it work. Luckily, the later it got, the better the chance I'd find him in homeroom.

He wasn't in homeroom. I paused in the doorway, looking around the class. I saw plenty of familiar faces, but none of them were Kurt's. I turned and leaned against the wall next to the entrance to the classroom. He'd show up eventually. He had to.

A minute or so later, I started worrying that maybe he wouldn't show up. He could be home sick today, after all, and there would be no way I'd know it. Nobody even knew I was standing out here waiting for him. But just as I was starting to think about giving up, I saw him off in the distance.

The good news was, he was alone.

I'd considered the possibility that he might come walking up with a crowd of guys and there would be nothing I could do about it. I wouldn't talk to him if there were people with him, so I'd just have to walk off and find him later. But he was walking all by himself, a totally serious look on his face. He looked more confident than ever, though, and I swore he looked like he was dressing better.

I bit my lip and stepped forward. This was a lot easier in my head. Face-to-face with him, I suddenly worried he'd think I was crazy or something.

This wasn't for me, I reminded myself. I had no interest in him. So this should be a breeze. But walking up to a boy you didn't know to tell him someone liked him wasn't as easy as it seemed like it would be.

I wasn't sure what to say as he approached, so instead I did something a little nutty. I stepped into the doorway of the classroom, blocking his path.

Understandably, he was thrown. He blinked at me, not speaking. He didn't seem to know what to say.

"Do you have a girlfriend?" I blurted. It was the first thing that popped into my head.

I realized as his expression changed even more—to one of wanting to run away—that he thought I was asking for myself. Like I was some kind of crazy stalkerish person who had tracked him down to demand to know if he had a girlfriend. I could see why that would be a little scary.

"Not for me," I said quickly. Wait. That didn't make sense. "I mean . . . someone else wants to know."

"Oh," Kurt said. He didn't look disappointed, just confused. Then he asked the question that more people should have asked when they found out some mysterious person liked them. "Who?"

Maybe it wasn't so bad that most people didn't ask who liked them. Should I tell him or keep it a mystery? I wasn't sure which would be better for making him walk a little straighter.

Then I remembered the point of all of this. I was trying to get Kurt and Sun together. The problem was, Sun was starting to look better—as Alex put it, she looked great. If she could get Kurt to take a long look at her, this could be phenomenal.

"Sun Patterson," I said. Then I waited for his eyes to light up.

He frowned. "Who?" he asked.

He really had no idea who she was. I thought about it a second. I guess that made sense. Sun had never really stood out like some other people around here. Same with Gillianni and, actually, same with Kurt. The rose had brought them out of their shells. Well, sort of.

"Sun Patterson," I said. "Long, dark hair and the prettiest eyes you've ever seen."

He looked even more confused. I guess it was good he didn't remember her. Maybe he'd see her and have no idea how she used to look.

"Oh, wait," he said. "Sun Patterson. Yeah. I think I know who she is."

Someone was standing behind Kurt, waiting to get into the classroom. We moved off to the side to stop blocking the entrance, and I considered my next words. I couldn't tell by looking at him what he thought of her.

So I asked.

"Do you think she's cute?" I asked.

He made a face; I'll just say it wasn't a *yes* face. It was the opposite. This wasn't helping.

"Have you seen her lately?" I asked. "She looks awesome. And she is a great girl."

He didn't look like he believed me. I couldn't blame him. But if I was going to play matchmaker for them, I needed to somehow get Kurt and Sun in the same place so he could see what she looked like. The question was . . . how?

"I have to get to class," Kurt said. He was looking pretty uncomfortable. All squirmy. I had to think fast.

"Lunch," I blurted excitedly. "I'll make sure you see what she looks like at lunch, 'kay?"

He wasn't even looking at me at that point. His attention was focused on that doorway. He looked really uncomfortable, too, like he couldn't wait to get away from me.

I was about to give up and walk away when suddenly I saw her in the distance. Sun Patterson. I didn't even stop to think about it, just shouted her name.

She was so far away, I had to yell pretty loud for her to hear me. That, of course, caught the attention of everyone in the area. Sun slowly turned, saw me, and waved. She even started toward me, but as she drew closer, she obviously spotted Kurt behind me, because her footsteps faltered.

"That's her," I said to Kurt. I spoke quickly, in case she decided to turn and run off in the other direction. "I can introduce you."

I turned to look at him and found him staring directly at her. He seemed impressed. His eyebrows were arched, and he had a very serious expression. I'd done it. My first match, all thanks to my rose trick. If I'd never sent the fake rose, Sun never would have started looking around at guys to decide she liked Kurt. She would have still been walking around, slumped over, her hair in her face so no one was able to see her beautiful eyes.

The bell rang, and I turned to start toward class. They'd seen each other. I could introduce them later. Now on to the next problem.

Who had put that rose in my locker?

CHAPTER NINE

♥

To: Ashleigh
From: Mia
It wouldn't hurt you to be nicer to people you don't know.

"Loser . . . and *loser*," Ashleigh said of Kurt and Sun. I'd been telling her and Alex about how I was trying to get Kurt and Sun together. She'd just labeled them "losers" and was taking a deep breath in preparation to move onto the next subject.

"Sun isn't a loser," Alex said.

"Neither is Kurt," I said, a little annoyed that Alex was defending Sun, probably because he thought she was "hot." Instead, though, they were now looking at me.

"Oh no," Ashleigh said. "Tell me you don't like Kurt. You can totally do better."

She rolled her eyes. Alex just stared at me as if he'd never seen me before. I, meanwhile, was staring at Ashleigh as if I'd never seen her before. Since when had she gotten so mean? What was going on here?

"I don't like Kurt," I said. "I don't like anyone."

"Mia doesn't believe in that stuff," Alex said with a shrug.

I didn't want to talk about any of that. It wasn't that I never wanted to go out with anyone—I just hadn't ever met anyone I liked. Instead of arguing about it, I decided to move on with my story.

"Anyway, I was thinking how cool it would be if I could get people together based on the roses," I said. "It would be like I'm Cupid."

Ashleigh gaped at me. "Seriously. Valentine's Day is over, so why don't you work on getting someone for you? You have to like someone by now."

I didn't, but I didn't have to tell the two of them that. "Maybe," I said. "I don't have to tell you if I do."

"Yes, you do," Ashleigh said. "It's BFF rule number one. We tell each other everything. I tell you everybody I like, and you tell me everybody you like."

"What about Alex?" I asked. He was watching both of us without saying a word.

"He likes Sun," Ashleigh said. "He told us that, which means you're the only one who isn't following the rules."

I thought about that a second. I wasn't a very good friend. A good BFF would never, ever keep her friend from getting the girl he liked. I felt a little sick. I had a plateful of yucky school cafeteria food in front of me, and I didn't think I could eat any of it.

"I forgot," I said.

It was a lie. And BFF rule number two was probably that we always had to tell the truth or something. Not that there were actual rules. It looked like we just made them up as we went along.

"Whatever," Alex said, and he didn't really look all that bothered by it.

Ashleigh sat up a little straighter. Her eyes were wide, and she was smiling that big smile that told me something must be up. She'd had another one of her great ideas.

"You should focus your efforts on getting Sun to like Alex," Ashleigh said.

She looked over at Alex, who seemed to be enjoying his cheeseburger. Apparently not caring if *he* cared or not, she continued.

"Think about it," she said. "It's perfect. You get to be a

matchmaker, and he gets to go out with the girl he likes. Win-win."

"It's no big deal," Alex said. "I like her, but whatever."

"See?" I asked. "He doesn't even like her that much. No problem."

Ashleigh looked at him briefly before turning back to me. "You're going to believe that? He wouldn't admit it if he wanted to marry her and give her a million dollars."

"A million dollars?" I asked. There had to be some way I could change the subject here. "Alex will never have a million dollars."

"A family down the street I think has a million dollars," Alex said.

I smiled. This was the kind of conversation Alex and I were used to. All this stuff about liking people and going out with people wasn't us at all. I just needed to shift the conversation back to normal stuff—

"What is it with you and all this matchmaking stuff anyway?" Ashleigh asked. "Why do you care?"

My smile fell. I hadn't planned on a question like that. I didn't have an answer for it. I hadn't really thought about it, but my sudden interest in helping everyone else had been kind of random.

"I like helping people," I said.

My mind was racing, trying to come up with some reason for playing Cupid. I think it all started with wanting to be as good as Kellie and Kaylee. But then, as I was selling roses to Kaylee and all her friends, I started thinking about how the same people got all the roses each year and the rest of us sat by watching. That was when it changed a bit. I knew there was no chance I'd get a rose, but wouldn't it be nice if people who never got attention got roses?

I wanted to see people even happier. It gave me something to do with my time, besides study, do homework, and talk on the phone to Alex and Ashleigh. It gave me a purpose.

But I couldn't explain all that. Ashleigh wouldn't understand. So I just told her part of the truth.

"It gives me something to do."

At least it was true. It wasn't the total truth, but Alex and Ashleigh would buy it. They knew I didn't have much going on.

"Join a club," Ashleigh said. "Try out for basketball with me."

Basketball. Yuck. We'd played basketball in gym and I'd made a complete fool of myself.

"You could join band," Alex said. "Or the school newspaper."

I frowned. What was wrong with what I was doing?

Making people happy was just as much of a hobby as playing a clarinet or dribbling a basketball. Actually, it was better.

"Or you could pick a boy you like and . . . *like* him," Ashleigh said. "Be your own matchmaker."

I looked over at Alex. He wasn't even looking at me anymore. I didn't really want his opinion on the issue. I actually wanted him to save me. He didn't seem like he was going to do that.

I had to save myself.

"Whatever," I said. Then, to Alex, I said, "Are you going to eat your pickles?"

The bell rang at that point, both keeping me from eating his pickles and getting me out of this conversation with Ashleigh. I grabbed my tray and jumped up, rushing toward the tray return. Ashleigh couldn't keep up with me, so she couldn't question me further. Or so I thought.

"I'll find *you* someone," Ashleigh said, rushing to follow me to my locker. "I'll be your matchmaker."

"No, thanks," I said. My locker was in sight. I just had to walk a little faster and I'd be there. . . .

"It'll be great," Ashleigh said. "You don't have to do anything. Just keep doing what you've been doing and I'll take care of the rest."

"Just leave her alone."

I was already at my locker when I heard Alex speak up. He was still off in the distance, but I could hear him. It stalled Ashleigh's progress for a second, which gave me time to get my books out. Maybe I could get to class while they argued it out.

"Nobody wants to be bugged about this stuff," Alex said. "In fact, I think people should just let everyone like who they want to like."

"Mia started it," Ashleigh argued. "I'm just doing what she's doing."

"Don't do that," he said.

"Don't you want to see her happy?" Ashleigh asked.

I slammed my locker shut. I wondered if I snuck around them and rushed off to class, how long it would take for them to notice I wasn't standing there anymore. Instead I turned to face them.

"I'm happy," I said. "I'm fine. Alex, will you walk to class with me?"

They both looked startled. I wanted to talk to Alex alone, but I didn't want Ashleigh to think I was mad at her.

"I just want to talk to him alone for a second," I said. "I'll see you after class, 'kay?"

She still looked confused, but she seemed to be gradually

recovering. She even smiled as she stepped back and waved good-bye. I knew Ashleigh. That meant she was up to something. I'd have to worry about that later.

"Let's go," Alex said.

He was getting impatient with all this like I was. I couldn't wait to get him alone so we could put things back to our normal weirdness. Anything was better than all this "people liking people" talk.

"Sorry about all that," I said once we were away from where she could hear us.

He didn't speak for several long seconds. I was starting to wonder if he was giving me the silent treatment. Then he spoke.

"You could have at least helped me with Sun," he said. "I thought we were friends."

I don't think I would have been more surprised if he'd said he was an alien. "I—I didn't know—"

"Of course you did. Ashleigh told you I like her. I tried to tell you, but you didn't want to hear it."

He'd tried to tell me? I thought back over the past week or two. We hadn't really talked, not like we used to. He barely spoke to me in anything more than a grunt. Had I somehow missed a conversation without realizing it?

"You tried to fix her up with someone else," he said. "That's the worst part of all of it."

"But she—"

I stopped myself before I could finish that sentence. Sun liked Kurt. She wanted me to talk to him for her. But if I said that now, it would just make Alex feel worse. So I didn't finish the sentence.

"What?" he asked.

Oh. He wasn't letting me off the hook that easily. I scrambled for an explanation.

"She doesn't know you like her," I said. "I don't think you want me to just come out and tell her, do you?"

"You don't have to do that," he said. "But fixing her up with someone else won't help at all."

"Good point," I said. I stopped and turned to face him. "Look, I'm sorry. I want to talk to you about all this, but it's just weird, you know? All my friends are getting crushes, and I'm—"

"Not," he finished for me. "Let Ashleigh help you then."

"I don't want Ashleigh to help," I said. "I want . . ."

I didn't have a way to finish that sentence either. Again, we were back to what I wanted.

"You want things to stay the same," he said. "All of

us just hanging out, not worrying about all this stuff. If that's the case, then why are you trying to get everyone else together?"

That was an easy question to answer. I could get Sun and Kurt together because they weren't my friends. I wouldn't lose them once they started going out. If I could get Alex and Sun together, that meant if we ever did talk, all we'd talk about was Sun.

I don't know how I knew all that. I just knew.

"Hey, guys."

I was still in the process of figuring out what I would say next when I heard another voice beside us. Not just any voice, though. The voice of Sun Patterson.

She was smiling at me. As I watched, she glanced over at Alex, giving him that same smile before turning back toward me.

She didn't seem to have overheard our conversation, but why was she here? Oh no. She wasn't here to ask if I'd talked to Kurt lately. Not in front of Alex. Not now.

"Big announcement about the rose sale coming up," she said, pointing toward the ceiling where the speakers were. Good. She hadn't brought up the whole Kurt thing.

"I have to get to class," Alex said.

He was backing away, and I knew any second he'd turn and rush off down the hallway, leaving me with no way to find out why he was mad at me. So I yelled out my question.

"Are we good?" I asked him.

He turned, looked at me, and shrugged, then rushed off toward class. I tried to remember a time in all the years I'd known Alex that we'd been mad at each other. I couldn't.

I headed into class feeling worse than I had in a long, long time.

But then something happened that perked me up. I was taking my seat when the final bell rang. My heart started pounding when I remembered what Sun Patterson had said. How had she known about the announcement? I thought about it. It made sense. It always took a couple days for the office to tally numbers for something like this. Maybe Sun had just guessed.

But then I caught a girl's eye who I barely knew. She was smiling at me. I realized several people were looking at me and talking. The office should have known that nothing that happens at Stanton Middle School ever stays secret for long.

"May I have your attention please?" the all-too-familiar voice of Kaylee Hooper boomed through the tiny, old speakers above our heads. "I have a big announcement about the Valentine's Day rose sale."

I was holding my breath. And people were still staring at me. If we'd lost, they wouldn't be looking at me like that. If we'd lost, I'd have to wonder what rumor was spreading about me that would have everyone staring at me like they were all in on a joke about me.

"It was a record year for rose sales," Kaylee said. "But one group of students outsold everyone else for the second year in a row. The seventh-grade class sold the most roses, winning the lock-in at the Rock 'N' Roll Sportsplex. Congratulations, seventh grade, and a special thanks to the committee for working so hard."

The committee. Not Ashleigh and me, who had sat at that table every morning, but the committee. All that work, and I was still mostly invisible.

That was okay, though. Everyone in seventh grade knew I'd done a lot of the work, and I was glad not to be recognized. Because really what I'd done had been borderline cheating. Sure, I'd sold the roses to myself and given them to other people. It wasn't like I'd put extra money in there without buying anything. And there was no rule against the committee buying roses—in fact, several of the members had lined up to buy roses the first day they were on sale. But I still felt like I didn't deserve a lot of credit because I'd bought so many of them myself.

Now that the announcements were over, people started reaching over to pat me on the back. There was a lot of "Congratulations" and "Way to go." I was surprised that I didn't feel more excited about it. It was, after all, the moment I'd worked so hard to have. Why did I have all this guilt?

And what could I do to make it go away?

CHAPTER TEN

❤

To: Mom
From: Mia
Everyone has to grow up sometime . . . even me.

"Are you sure it's safe?" Mom asked. Mom had just gotten home from work. She'd barely walked through the door when I'd broken the news about the lock-in.

It was so weird. Mom had been excited about the lock-in until I'd won. Now she was worried about me staying all night in a strange place.

"Mia worked hard selling those roses," Kellie said. "She deserves her reward."

Go, Kellie!

Mom looked at Kellie, a frown firmly set on her face. "We don't even know if there will be chaperones there," she told her.

"I'm sure there are chaperones." Kellie looked at me. "There are chaperones, right?"

I shrugged. "I guess."

I mean, there had to be teachers, right? I didn't want to think about that part of it. I was having a hard enough time figuring out how I'd keep Alex and Sun apart. And Alex and Kurt apart. And Sun and Kurt apart so Alex didn't get mad about them being together.

"Lock-ins are cool," Kellie said, biting into her after-school, pre-game apple. She just said stuff like that to make me feel better, since she was doing things I wouldn't be able to do for at least a couple of years. By then, she'd be doing even cooler things that I wouldn't be able to do.

"What will you be doing?" Mom asked. "At the lock-in."

I shrugged. "Hanging out." We didn't really have to *do* anything. Just being there all night would be awesomeness.

"Will you be sleeping or staying up all night?" Mom asked. "Going without sleep isn't so easy when you really try it."

"I've stayed up all night before," I said. "My sleepover last year."

Mom laughed. "As I recall, I checked in on you around two a.m. and found you were all snoozing away."

I was hoping she'd forgotten that. "We'll have stuff to do to keep us busy," I said. "Plus, there won't be anywhere to sleep."

"She can nap beforehand," Kellie said. "Let her have fun."

"I still remember my first lock-in," Mom said, getting that look in her eye.

Kellie and I looked at each other. If this was heading down the road of, *Oh, I remember my first lock-in*, I wanted to excuse myself now.

Sure enough, Mom started. It happened in fifth grade, when she'd spent the night in a church that had a special screen on which they showed old black-and-white movies. I was wondering how long this torture would continue when my cell phone rang.

"It's about homework," I blurted, grabbing my phone.

Luckily, her trip down memory lane had her occupied long enough for me to get to the hallway. I don't know if she even noticed I'd left. I glanced at the screen and saw a number I didn't recognize.

"Hello?" I asked, mashing the button before it could kick over to my voice mail.

"It's Sun," the voice on the other end said. "Sun Patterson."

She didn't have to say her last name. It wasn't like there were a million people named Sun in our school. But the one

Sun I did know didn't call me. Ever. She must have gotten my phone number from someone on the rose committee. When you work on a committee, apparently your cell number becomes public information.

Eager to hear what this was all about, I headed down the hallway, cell phone pressed tightly to my ear. "What's up?" I asked when I was far enough away that no one could hear.

"I need your help," Sun said.

"Okay," I said. I needed to sit down. I headed into my bedroom and flopped down on the bed.

"I need a makeover," she said. "I have to do something to get Kurt's attention. I have money, but I don't know anyone else with, you know . . ."

"Free time?" I asked, figuring anyone else she'd ask would be busy. She probably had already asked seventeen people or something before she even thought of calling me.

"Taste," she said. "You always wear cute clothes and stuff. I want to do that too."

This was all very, very weird. Maybe someone was playing a trick on me.

"I just need you to meet me tomorrow at the mall," she said. "Do you have plans?"

Tomorrow was Saturday. I was hanging out at Ashleigh's

house tonight to get out of Kellie's game, but I had no plans for tomorrow.

This was my chance. I'd messed things up with Alex, and now, hanging out at the mall with Sun, I'd be able to put in a good word for him. "Let me talk to my mom and call you back," I said.

I walked back to the dining room and asked if I could go to the mall with Sun tomorrow.

"No," Mom said. "I'm not comfortable with you hanging out at the mall without an adult to supervise."

"Mom," Kellie said, rolling her eyes. "She's old enough. Plus, the only people who hang out at the mall are old ladies and people Mia's age."

I started to feel offended by that, but Kellie was actually on my side. I kept my mouth shut while I waited for Mom's answer.

"Old ladies?" Mom asked her. "I beg your pardon. I'm not old."

Kellie seemed to realize she'd said the wrong thing. Before she could make it worse, I jumped in.

"I'll get Sun's mom to take us and pick us up," I begged, looking directly at Mom now. "You won't have to do anything."

She said yes.

Of course, that meant I had to get Sun to talk her mom into doing all the work. I sent her a text this time. Texting was the best way to deal with people you didn't know all that well.

Sun texted back, NO PROB. WILL PICK YOU UP. Of course, Mom came to my room later that night to tell me she had to meet Sun and her mom before I could go.

Totally embarrassing. I wanted to invite Ashleigh along, but I knew better. Even if I could get her to agree to go, she'd take all the fun out of it.

During movie night, I kept my mouth shut. I listened to Ashleigh talk about Sun and Alex and how we could get them together and said nothing, even though it was bothering me for reasons I didn't understand. All I knew was that it bothered me that it bothered me.

Sun's mom was picking me up at one o'clock. Late enough so we wouldn't have to eat lunch together but early enough that we wouldn't have to worry about dinner together. I was no dummy. I knew how all this worked. In fact, I probably would have done the same if I was the one planning things.

At one o'clock on the dot, they pulled up in the driveway and honked the horn. Mom gave me a look, then tossed the front door open and gestured for me to head out ahead of her. She didn't like the whole "honk the horn" thing when someone picked me up. She'd made that clear more than once. But I didn't really have control of what Sun Patterson's mother did.

Mom followed me up the driveway, stepping up next to me at the driver's-side window of Sun's mom's car. Her mom had one of those nice little sports cars that looked like it wouldn't seat more than a couple of people, but it had a backseat, way back there. It was small, but I'd fit.

Out of the corner of my eye, though, I could see Mom's frown. She didn't like tiny backseats, either. Mom needed to learn to be more flexible.

Speaking of flexible . . .

Sun stepped out of the car and held her door open. She looked like she always looked. Her hair was straight but frizzy. Tiny little hairs flew all over the place—

"I'll just hang out at the food court until they're finished," I heard Sun's mom say as I climbed into the backseat.

What? She was going into the mall with us?

Not cool. Not cool at all.

As I settled in and Sun sat down, trapping me in my seat, I realized that I was doomed if someone from school was at the mall anyway. They'd see me with Sun and tell everyone else. Ashleigh would flip out and maybe even be too embarrassed to be seen with me. The only good thing was that we were going to a dead mall that nobody went to anymore. Everyone I knew shopped at the Forever 21 in the fancy part of town these days. But the mall was the only place someone could get a haircut, makeup, and clothes in one place, and all of those were things Sun needed.

"Keep your cell phone on," Mom said as Sun's mom kicked it into reverse and started backing out of the driveway. "Be home before five. Pizza."

She yelled that last part out, which was humiliating, to say the least. I shrank down in the seat a little, trying to hide behind Sun's dinky seat. There was no hiding in a car like this.

Sun's mom sped off. I winced and looked out of the back window. Sure enough, Mom was standing there, arms crossed.

"It's so nice of you to do this for Sun," her mom said. "I know how much it means to her."

"Mom!" Now it was Sun's turn to shrink down in her seat.

"What?" Sun's mom looked over at her daughter, and the car swerved to the right slightly. I covered my mouth to keep a gasp from coming out. "You haven't been out with friends since last year. I think it's good you're finally starting to meet people."

Wow. Awkward. I rushed to change the subject.

"Mrs. Patterson—" I began.

"MacDowell," Sun interrupted.

Sun's mom must have seen my confused look in the rear-view mirror. "My last name is MacDowell," she said. "That's Sun's stepdad's last name."

"Oh." I hadn't known Sun's dad wasn't her dad. I wondered when they'd gotten divorced. There were a lot of kids who'd been through their parents divorcing when we were in elementary school, but nobody I hung out with. I wondered when they'd split up and if that was why Sun was so quiet.

"Mrs. MacDowell," I corrected. "Can Sun get a haircut?" It was the first thing I thought of, inspired mostly through spotting Sun's flyaway hairs in front of me.

But Sun sat up straight in her seat. "Not my hair," she said. "No."

"I think that would be a great idea," Mrs. MacDowell said. She addressed this to me, completely bypassing her daughter, who was now staring at her with her jaw hanging. "You'd look really cute with a bob. In fact, I'll make an appointment for you now."

While Mrs. MacDowell spent two minutes trying to force the voice activation in her car to dial mall information, Sun spun all the way around in her seat to glare at me. "*What are you doing?*" she whispered.

"You said you wanted a makeover," I whispered back. "We should start with your hair."

"I wanted some cute clothes. That's all."

"Trust me," I said. I gave her a big smile, which she, of course, didn't return before spinning back around to face front. Her mother, meanwhile, had managed to get the nice lady who answered at the mall to connect her with someplace called Express Hair and Nails.

"Express," Sun said. "Doesn't that mean fast? I don't think that's a good quality for a hair place to have."

I laughed. Now that I heard her actually talk, I found I was starting to like Sun. She wasn't some weird person who never spoke. She was . . . nice. Even maybe a little cooler than other people at our school.

"I'd like to make an appointment," Mrs. MacDowell shouted up at the roof of her car. That was where the microphone was, right above her head. I wondered if she realized she didn't have to yell to be heard. "Two o'clock for Sun Patterson. Throw in a cut for Mia— What's your last name, dear?"

"Hartley," I said quietly.

"Hartley," Mrs. MacDowell yelled.

So there we were, with two appointments. I tugged at the ends of my hair—probably split—and wondered what kind of haircut I'd get from a place whose biggest marketing tool was announcing it was "express." Like a fast-food drive-through.

Mrs. MacDowell let us off at the food court with a promise to be back to get us at three thirty. I followed Sun through the big automatic-open doors and caught up with her inside.

"I thought she planned to wait for us at the food court," I commented.

"Huh?" Sun was looking around like she'd suddenly been released into the wild. "Oh, that. She just said that to make your mom happy."

What? My mom would have a freak-out fit if she found out Mrs. MacDowell lied. I didn't know how she'd ever find out unless she randomly showed up here to stalk us, but still it was risky. Plus, whose parents lied? Mine didn't do things like that, *especially* to other parents or teachers. I thought there were rules against things like that.

"My mom has a busy schedule," Sun said. "She's a real estate agent." As if that were supposed to mean something to me. "Ooh, accessories."

Accessories were not what we needed right now. Cute earrings and clinky bracelets would be useless if paired with a zipped-up hoodie and baggy men's jeans. I couldn't tell her that, though. She was in the store before I could catch up with her.

She headed toward a rack of rubber bracelets, but I steered her back to something more feminine. I only had to use the words "trust me" seven or eight times before she finally agreed to buy a bunch of silver bracelets, some pink crystal earrings, and a cute sparkly hair tie for holding her hair down.

We were about to deal with that, anyway. But first we stopped off at the only teen clothing place I could find. It wasn't Forever 21, but close enough.

"Trust me," I said, holding up a short-sleeved pink shirt. The color brought out the natural highlights in her hair, and I had a feeling it would look even better once she got a haircut.

"It's cold outside," she said.

"So?"

She looked at the shirt. "That's short-sleeved."

"So?" I wasn't deliberately being difficult. I really didn't know what her point was.

"So I don't wear short sleeves when it's cold," she said.

"You wear a jacket over it." I turned around and, spotting a hoodie a few racks away, ran over to grab it. As I rushed back to her, she stared at the hoodie in horror.

"That's not a jacket," she said. "That's a hoodie."

"It's a jacket. Trust me. Try it on."

I thrust it out to her, and she tentatively took it. I then pointed to the dressing room and continued looking for more tight short-sleeved tops while she skulked off. I knew exactly what she was thinking. Sun was one of those girls with a great figure who hid behind big, bulky coats and baggy clothes all winter. While that kept her warm, it didn't flatter her. The goal here was to get her out of the background and up where everyone could see how awesome she was. First steps were cute clothes and *no* coats.

"I'll freeze," she said when I returned to her dressing room, knocked on the door, and demanded she show me the outfit. She wore the shirt and jacket with her baggy jeans, so it was hard to tell.

"You'll be fine," I said. "Try these on."

I handed her a stack of cute skinny jeans in every size I thought might fit, along with a stack of shirts, and stepped back. This was kind of fun.

My cell phone rang the second after Sun closed the dressing room door. It was Ashleigh. I stared at the screen for a long time, debating what to do. If I answered, I'd have to tell her where I was. She'd freak out if I told her I was with Sun Patterson, but I couldn't lie to her.

Could I?

Turns out, I could.

"Hello?" I whispered. I was walking away from the dressing room, but I was still afraid Sun would hear me.

"What's up?" she asked. "I'm bored."

"Just waiting for my mom at the grocery store," I said, wincing. I hated lying to my BFF. I felt like she could see me through the cell phone signals. "You coming over tonight? It's pizza night."

"Sure," she said. "I was wondering if I could come over a little early, though. We could hang out and chat before dinner."

"I'm not sure how long we're going to be," I said. Even as

I said the words, I was hoping with all I had that she wouldn't creep over to my house early. If she saw my mom's car in the driveway, she'd know I was lying. "Mom has a lot of errands to run."

If we really were at the grocery store, we'd have to go straight home. We'd have ice cream and frozen peas and milk—all of which would have to get to the refrigerator and freezer instead of being carried around town in Mom's trunk while she went everywhere. But luckily, Ashleigh didn't seem to think about any of that.

"Just call me when you get home," she said. "Alex may come over."

Alex lived a few streets over from Ashleigh, but they never, ever hung out without me. I felt a pang of jealousy at the thought of him going to her house and me not being there. But I couldn't blame her. I was hanging out with someone completely different, after all.

"Okay," I said . . . because there was nothing else I could say. If I was going to help the population of Stanton Middle School, my friends' lives would go on without me. What else could I expect?

"Can I stop trying on clothes now?"

Sun had snuck up on me so suddenly, I didn't have a

chance to prepare. I spun around to find her standing there, empty-armed, wearing the clothes she'd been wearing when this whole shopping outing had started.

"Who's that?" I heard Ashleigh say through the earpiece of my phone. "I thought you were at the grocery store."

"Um . . . yeah," I said. "That's . . . my sister. We're at Mega-Mart."

Mega-Mart was the big grocery-store-slash-department-store in town. It was totally possible we'd gone shopping with Mom and now were trying on clothes.

"That's not your sister," Ashleigh said. "Whatever. I'll talk to you later."

I still had my mouth open to argue with her when the phone went silent. I looked at the screen and saw CALL ENDED on the screen right above the photo I'd taken of her so her face would flash whenever she called. I'm not sure how long I stood there, staring at that flashing photo, before Sun waved her hand in front of me.

"Hello?" Sun said. "You in there?"

I looked up and nodded numbly while pocketing my phone. I'd just have to find a way to deal with Ashleigh later. We had a hair appointment to get to.

"Where are your clothes?" I asked Sun.

"In there." She pointed at the dressing room she'd just exited. I followed her pointing finger before looking back at her again.

"You aren't buying any of them?" I asked.

She wrinkled her nose. "They aren't me," she said. "I think I should stick with the clothes I have already."

I crossed my arms over my chest. Oh no. I was not going to waste an entire Saturday on this and possibly make my best friend mad for her to walk away with the same horrible wardrobe she'd been wearing forever.

But then again . . . if she didn't change her clothes, she wouldn't look better. If she didn't look better, Alex wouldn't like her more.

That thought flew through my mind so fast, it shocked me. I stopped, thought about it a second, and frowned. Whoa, that was harsh. I immediately felt bad for even thinking that.

"I see," I said, not budging even though I could tell she was practically jumping out of those boy clothes to rush around me and get out of here. "Humph. I guess I was wrong."

She stopped eyeing the exit anxiously and looked at me. "Wrong about what?"

I shrugged. "You. I thought you wanted a makeover. I thought that was what this was all about."

She looked down. I saw all the happiness go out of her and felt really, really bad.

"I just don't think I can wear that stuff," she said. "It's just not me."

What was she talking about? Every shirt and pair of pants I'd given her would look good on her. I just knew they would. Surely that wasn't what she was talking about.

"You look great," I said. "But buy the jackets, too. Then if you feel self-conscious at first, you can wear the jacket, right? Eventually you'll feel comfortable leaving the jacket in your locker."

She lifted her head and looked thoughtfully off to the side. I was getting through to her. Hallelujah!

We sorted through the stack and found five shirts and a great-fitting pair of jeans for her to buy. I would have bought more, just to have more than one pair of pants to switch out, but it was her money, so I couldn't tell her that.

While Sun paid, I nervously fumbled with my cell. I could call Ashleigh while we were waiting, but what would I tell her? I had to come up with a good excuse for why I was trying on clothes with someone who wasn't my sister . . . or her.

Ashleigh would believe me and get over it. She had to.

CHAPTER ELEVEN

❤

To: Mia
From: Ashleigh
Friends don't lie.

"What's with your hair?"

I was standing on Alex's porch, trying to get to Ashleigh. I'd rushed Sun through her haircut and mine to get here faster. I didn't even really care about my new, shoulder-length hairdo that the stylist had curled with a dryer and round brush until it was sticking up high from my head like someone from the eighties.

I patted the top down with my hand as I rose up on tiptoe to try to see past Alex.

"Is she here?" I asked.

"She's busy right now," Alex said.

When I lowered back down, I saw he wasn't meeting my eyes. I knew he was lying.

I could take Alex, though. I pushed past him and into the house, where Ashleigh was camped out in the kitchen, surrounded by junk food.

I felt a pang. This was what I was missing. This time with my BFFs, eating junk food and talking about people at school. I was giving it up . . . for what? To help some girl who wasn't even grateful for her new, kick-butt hairstyle that I'd talked her into getting?

"I'm here," I said, trying to keep my voice light. Maybe if I acted like nothing had happened, she'd forget about everything and we could go back to the way we'd been last night.

"Right," she said, turning her back on me to open the refrigerator door. "Who were you shopping for clothes with?"

I paused. "Sun Patterson," I said. Best to be honest.

Ashleigh let the refrigerator door slam shut and turned to look at Alex. "Really." She rolled her eyes and shook her head. Finally she turned to look at me. "You've been with Sun Patterson all afternoon?"

I nodded. Why did I have a bad feeling about all this?

"And you didn't invite me."

Ashleigh looked at me now, right in the eye. I felt like shrinking back against the wall.

"I—I didn't really have time—" I stopped. I was stuttering. It wasn't helping my case at all.

"When did she invite you?" Ashleigh asked. "Because I heard she called you yesterday to ask."

I stopped to think. How would word have gotten out so quickly? Sun. Sun must have told people. But who? And why?

"She told me she was going shopping with you today," Alex said. "We talked last night."

I'm not sure how long I stood there, staring at Alex like I'd never seen him before. He and Sun were all the way to "phone" status? That was huge. That was, like, one step away from dating.

"She asked for my help," I said, still staring at Alex. "She wanted to look better. I didn't think you would want to go."

For that last part, I turned back to Ashleigh. I didn't have to say it, did I?

I leaned forward, speaking in as low a voice as I could, even though Alex could probably hear. "I was trying to make her look better for Alex. It was a surprise."

"Stop," Ashleigh interrupted, holding up her hand, palm

facing me. "I don't care if you have new friends. That's fine. But if you don't want to hang out with us anymore, you can just tell us. You don't have to lie."

"Ashleigh—" Alex said. He looked at me. "She's just hurt because you didn't invite her. I'm sure—"

"I think we've said all we need to say to her, Alex," she interrupted. "Come on." She marched toward Alex, stopping just in front of him. He looked at me apologetically before turning and walking from the room ahead of her. Somehow, in one afternoon, I'd managed to lose my two best friends in the world because of my lies. And they didn't even know about the biggest lie of all—the roses.

If I was worried about having someone to talk to at school Monday, I didn't have to worry long. I was standing in the hallway outside homeroom, hoping Alex or Ashleigh would happen by, when suddenly I found myself surrounded.

Trudie Kepler and her friends had ambushed me. And they were making zero sense.

"We just saw Sun Patterson," one of the girls said. She put a hand on each hip. "We want that."

"I want mine blond."

"I want pink lipstick. The glossy kind."

As her friends carried on nonsensically, Trudie said absolutely nothing. She just stared at me, studying me with her beady brown eyes. It was making me more than a little nervous.

"What?" I asked her, shutting out all the other chatter around us.

"I want what you did for Sun Patterson," Trudie said. She stepped a little closer to me. I would have backed up, but my back was already against the wall. "Except I don't want to change my hair."

Interesting. Because her hair was one of the first things I would have changed if someone asked. There had to be a better way than wearing it in a ponytail every day.

"Me too." One by one, each of her friends expressed their desire for a Sun Patterson–style makeover. I just continued to stare at Trudie in the hopes that they'd all give up and go away.

"Oh, and I don't have money for new clothes," Trudie said.

I waited for the round of "me toos" on that one, but none came. Instead they each started offering to let her borrow money. Someone said she could go to a used clothing store, and someone else said she could get diseases from wearing someone else's clothing. Meanwhile, people were trying to push past them to get into the classroom. It was a mess.

"You'll need new clothes," I said. Then I realized that wasn't a very nice thing to say. "No offense."

"None taken," Trudie said. I was shocked she was okay with that. "I know I don't have much to work with here, but we don't have the money for thousands of dollars in new clothes."

"There's a great discount clothing store in the shopping center where the thrift store is," I said. "There's a ton of cute stuff. You'll love it, and it won't cost a fortune."

"Great," Trudie said. She smiled. Well, what passed for a smile on her face, anyway, which was more like a look of pain. "So you'll come with?"

"Come with?" I asked. She was missing an object in that sentence, as I knew from grammar class. I kind of knew what she was asking, so I was hiding behind grammar to avoid it.

"Come with me," Trudie said, shaking her head slightly as if I should know that already. "I can't do this alone."

I couldn't do it with her. I mean, I could, but my two closest friends were already mad at me for helping someone out with her wardrobe, hair, and makeup. I couldn't spend every spare second I had following people around to shopping centers and handing them clothes over dressing room doors.

"I can't," I said. "I have plans."

"I didn't even say when," Trudie said.

Oh. Oops.

"I assumed you meant today after school," I said. "I have plans. It's a . . . homework thing."

"No," Trudie said. "I have soccer practice after school. It'll have to be this weekend. You name the time."

Just as I was forming some big, detailed story about how I had to go out of town this weekend, one of the "me too" people spoke up.

"Or any weekend after that," the girl said. "You name the time and place. We'll be there."

We'll be there? Did that mean all these people were coming to the store too? I didn't know about that. I wondered if I had the right to speak up and say no to that plan.

"Just us," Trudie said, flashing a dirty look at her friend. "I think Mia can handle this."

I was so grateful Trudie had called off the hounds, I blurted, "Okay" before I realized it. Trudie accepted it, said, "Thanks," and spun on one heel to stalk off.

Suddenly Sun Patterson appeared by my side. "You have to help me," she said. The warning bell rang and people began rushing off to class behind her. Sun looked up anxiously at the speaker that carried the sound. "I'll be back here after homeroom and we'll walk together."

I didn't have time to argue that I had no extra time between homeroom and first period. Basically, I could only just get to my locker, get my books, and run to my first class before the bell rang. I'd just have to rush and Sun would figure it out.

I plopped down in my seat, which was next to Alex's empty desk. He was supposed to be here. I was going to talk to him and smooth things over between us before class. Where was he?

The final bell rang and still no Alex. Had he stayed home sick today because of what happened with all of us this weekend? Had Ashleigh stayed home too?

I got my answer a few seconds later when he came rushing in. He slid into his seat but didn't look at me. He stared straight ahead, unblinking, even as I refused to look away. I had to be able to get his attention somehow so I could talk to him.

When he wouldn't look at me, I got an idea. I ripped out a tiny square of paper from my notebook and wrote a note to him.

Alex,

Please don't be mad at me. I miss hanging out with you. Just us.

Mia

Before I could lose my courage, I folded it and handed it over to him. He didn't look at me, so I set it on top of his book. He'd have to read it now. Knowing Alex, he'd wait until he was in his next class, where I couldn't see him, and open it.

I tried to forget about Alex as I pretended to pay attention to some lecture on a canned food drive. I even took notes. But I was secretly writing a list in the left column of my notepaper, detailing the things I could do to win Alex back.

The bell rang as I was halfway through writing idea number seven in tiny print that nobody could read but me. It caught me unprepared, making me forget I was supposed to walk with Alex and convince him he had to speak to me. I hopped up, scooping my books up with me, but then I forgot my purse, which was hanging on the back of my chair. By the time I returned, grabbed my purse, and left the classroom, Alex was long gone.

But Sun was waiting outside the door.

Ugh.

"You ready?" Sun asked.

I said, "Sure," as I kept walking.

The last thing I needed right now was to hear how much Sun liked Kurt. I couldn't help her get him now. I couldn't even get my BMFF to take a note from me. Strange how, for some reason, I was more upset by Alex being mad than Ashleigh. Ashleigh was my super BFF. What was up with the whole Alex thing? I didn't get it.

"I need you to help me with a guy thing."

I gave her a quick look as we pushed our way through a crowd that had gathered around Kaylee. "That's your emergency?" I asked. I hated to say it, but I was relieved it wasn't about Alex.

"Emergency?" she asked. She must not have realized how desperate the tone of her voice sounded. "No. I just really need your help. It's something only you can help me with."

I headed straight for my locker. My mind raced. What excuse could I give? I had to get away from Sun as quickly as possible. If Ashleigh or Alex saw me talking to her, it would only make things worse.

"I have to get to class," I said. "There's this big test—"

My locker pulled open too easily. Frowning, I looked at the door. Something was weird.

Sun said something, but I didn't hear it because a foil object struck me in the forehead. It took me a second to figure out what was going on, but as I reached down and my hand grasped a familiar plastic stem, I realized what had been left inside my locker.

Another chocolate rose.

It was just like the other one. I could hear Sun talking to me and knew I had to pull out of this trance, but for the longest time, all I could do was stand there, staring at it.

Where were these roses coming from?

CHAPTER TWELVE

❤

To: Stanton Middle School

From: Mia

I am not your personal stylist.

"Hello? Mia? Mia!"

I looked over at Sun. Even with all her babbling, she was staring at the rose in my hand.

"What's that?" she asked.

"A rose," I said.

Sun wrinkled her nose. "From Valentine's Day? I wouldn't eat it. It's probably bad by now. Anyway, can you help me?"

"Hmm?" I asked, distracted. I had no idea what I was agreeing to do.

"'Kay," she said excitedly. "I'll walk with you."

"Wait. What?" I had no idea what was going on.

"You aren't listening," Sun said, looking down at the rose in my hand. "What does the card say?"

My fingers fumbled with the card as I tried to open it. My hands were shaking—I was shaking all over. Just when I'd almost forgotten about the first rose, here was another one. What did it mean?

I leaned against my locker to steady myself a little before sliding the card open. . . .

"Hey, isn't that your friend?" Sun asked.

I looked up to see her looking past me. I followed her stare. Sure enough, just a few feet away was Ashleigh, walking right in our direction. Alex was nowhere in sight, but he didn't have to be. Ashleigh's expression showed me all the disapproval she was feeling at seeing me standing at my locker with Sun.

I couldn't believe I'd upset my best friend by lying to her. And I was only making it worse by hanging out with Sun. Now she'd probably think I'd decided I'd rather hang out with Sun than her *all* the time.

Before I could figure out what to do, it was already too late. Ashleigh had already breezed right past me, narrowing her eyes at me before looking away. My best friend, the one who had been with me through so much, was now glaring at me when she walked by.

"What's up with that?" Sun asked. She turned back around without waiting for an answer. "Anyway, so I need someone's attention. You can help me."

I heard Sun talking, but I didn't really hear what she was saying. To me, it was all babble. How could I worry about Sun's self-consciousness when my whole world was falling apart?

"Can you help me?" Sun asked. She was definitely a persistent little thing.

"Huh? Oh, I don't know. I really have a lot going on right now. Everyone wants me to help them look like you. It's all kind of . . . crazy right now. Not that people wanting to look like you is crazy."

Ugh. Now I was the one babbling. I was a mess. And I *still* hadn't looked at the card. I tore it off the rose and shoved it into my pocket. I'd read it later.

"People want to look like me?" Sun asked, surprised.

Tossing the rose into my locker, I closed the door and started walking.

"Who?" Sun asked, chasing after me. "Did they say that, specifically?"

"Not specifically." Wait, that wasn't true. "Well, yes, specifically. Trudie said she wanted to look like you."

"Trudie Kepler?" Sun asked. "The soccer player?"

I knew what she was thinking from the look on her face. Trudie Kepler was about as far from looking like Sun Patterson as she could get. She had the build of a linebacker, and her hair was a frizzball she always wore in a ponytail. There was no way humanly possible to make the two girls look alike ever.

"She just meant that she saw how you looked and it gave her hope," I said with a shrug. I was looking around nervously, worried Alex would pass by, making things worse. Not that they could get any worse at this point. "She wants me to do whatever it is she thinks I did for you."

"You did this," Sun said. She gestured to indicate herself from head to toe.

"Part of it," I said. "You did the rest. It isn't really about the way you look. It's that you have confidence. They think clothes and makeup will do that. Maybe it will."

With a half wave, I backed toward the classroom. She was seriously about to follow me.

"You didn't hear what I need help with," she said. "It's about this guy."

The warning bell rang, and people started pushing past us to get to their seats. I figured being quiet was the best way to get her to hurry up and spit out whatever she was trying to say. What else could I do? I'd already told Kurt Barnes she liked him. I'd helped bring out her confidence so he'd notice her.

"He'll be at the lock-in Friday," she said. "I wanted to see if you could help get us together."

"No," I said.

The word came out before I had time to think about it. It sounded rude, and I wanted to take it back, especially when I saw the hurt look on her face. But if I did one more thing to help get Sun and Kurt together, Alex would really never speak to me again. And I wanted my friend back. If anything, I had to try to keep Sun and Kurt apart.

So why did the idea of getting Sun and Kurt together sound like a good plan after all?

I shook off that thought and said, "I can't do it all for you, Sun. It's your turn. You have to do the work from here."

With that, I turned around and walked into my class. By the time I sat down and looked at the doorway, Sun was gone.

That was when I realized I still hadn't read my card. I pulled it from my pocket and was about to open it when

Mrs. Templeton started speaking. I swear she was looking straight at me.

The sudden image of her possibly confiscating the card and never letting me see it or, worse, reading its contents out loud in front of the whole class sent me into a panic. I tucked the card inside the front cover of my book and didn't look at it again until the end of class.

When the bell rang, the classroom emptied out. I opened the book and, finally, the card. I had to know what it said.

I read and reread the words several times before I finally processed them. I'd been right. This message was worse than the first one.

To: Mia
From: Your Secret Admirer
I know what you did. I'm going to tell.

CHAPTER THIRTEEN

♥

To: My Secret Admirer

From: Mia

What do you want from me?

"Miss Hartley? Is there a problem?"

Mrs. Templeton was standing nearby, staring me down. Oh, right. I was still sitting at my desk after the entire place had cleared out. The next class was already starting to trickle in. No wonder she was worried about me.

"No, no problem." I shoved the card into my pocket and stood, sweeping up my books as I headed for the door. I felt like I'd been caught doing something horrible, but really, she wouldn't know what this card was. It was between classes, so it wasn't like I was breaking some rule by looking at it.

"Okay, well, time to get to your next class," she said. "Tardiness is not appreciated at Stanton Middle School."

Yeah, yeah. Whatever. I sped from the room and headed straight for my locker.

"Me again."

I sighed before I could stop myself. Realizing that was rude, I held my breath, forced a big smile, and spun around.

"I need your help," Sun said. "Walk with me."

I opened my mouth to protest, but she was already walking. I rushed to catch up with her, trying to think of an excuse for why we didn't need to have this conversation again.

"Fine, I'll help," I said.

While we walked, I was looking around. I was paranoid about seeing Ashleigh, but that was only a small part of it. Mostly, my mind was running over the words on that card: *I know what you did. I'm going to tell.*

It could be anyone. I watched my classmates walk past. Most weren't paying attention to me at all, but that didn't mean anything. It probably meant the person had been watching me when I was selling flowers in the cafeteria. How would they know about the fake list I made? I'd done that in the girls' restroom before school. Nobody could have been watching me, could they?

I thought about people who might have seen. Maybe

Kaylee or one of her friends had started to come in one of the doors and I hadn't noticed. Still, all anyone would have seen would have been me writing on the notepad. My sister could be playing a mean joke on me, but she didn't even go to this school. I doubted she'd go to the trouble of coming here to put roses in my locker or even bribing someone else to do it. It just wasn't her style.

Something else hit me. I almost stopped walking as the thought crossed my brain. *I know what you did* could mean anything. I'd done a lot of things in my life, and a few of them could be blackmail-worthy, if that was what this was all about. Still . . . none of them involved chocolate roses, which were what the cards with my fake notes had been attached to. There had to be something to that, right?

"I really need you to talk to someone for me."

This again? "I talked to Kurt," I said. "I tried to introduce you, but you didn't come over—"

"Not Kurt," she interrupted. "Someone else." She stopped, seeming to suddenly realize what I'd just said. "Wait, did you say you talked to Kurt about me?"

"Yes." I didn't have a good feeling about this.

"I wish you hadn't done that." She stopped, looking around nervously. "I changed my mind."

My eyebrows arched. "You changed your mind? About the boy you liked just a couple of days ago?"

"There's someone else I like now."

Maybe I just didn't know how this boy thing worked. I'd never liked a boy, unless you counted guys I saw on TV or heard on the radio. I thought when someone liked someone, they at least stuck with it for a few weeks.

But then I remembered the look on Kurt's face when I told him Sun liked him. He even made a face. This was probably for the best. Sun would never have to know he didn't like her.

"Who's the guy?" I asked.

"Actually, it's someone you know really well," Sun said. Her expression had already brightened considerably, just talking about him. "I see you with him all the time."

Oh. There was only one guy she could possibly see me with all the time. And that guy just happened to like her back.

"Alex," I said. There was that sick feeling again. Only this time it wasn't guilt that I'd tried to get in the way of Alex getting together with Sun. This time it was something else.

"Yes," Sun said. "Does he like anyone?"

"Look, I'm not sure I can help you much. He's kind of mad at me right now," I said.

"Why?"

I racked my brain for an answer to that question. "It was just a disagreement," I finally said, when I figured out I couldn't say anything about the real reason Alex and Ashleigh were mad at me. I mean, the truth was they were mad I was helping Sun. She would think that meant they didn't like her, which wouldn't be all that good for her feelings.

Except Alex liked Sun back. So maybe this was a way back to his good side.

"Okay," Sun said. "Well, if you guys get a chance to talk again, could you put in a good word for me?"

"Sure," I said. I gave her a big smile that showed far more confidence than I had. I had a feeling all I really needed to do was get Alex to listen to me for five seconds and this would turn it all around. He'd want to know more about what Sun had said about him. It would work, I just knew it.

I was plotting it all out in third period when Kaylee walked in, Rosalia chasing after her. They both looked at me, then each other. As they turned to walk toward their seats, they had huge smirks. Weird.

That was just the start of it. At first I thought it might be that threatening card, rubbing off on me. It seemed like everyone, everywhere I went, was staring at me. I wanted to crawl into one of these lockers and hide.

By the time I walked into lunch, I felt like everyone knew something I didn't. Even worse, for the first time since kindergarten, I was walking into the lunchroom with no idea who I would sit with.

I didn't want to sit alone. Everyone would stare at me even worse then. My bright idea was to plop down with Ashleigh and Alex and spill everything I knew about Sun. Once Alex knew Sun liked him, he would be more than happy to talk to me.

Only one problem with that. Ashleigh and Alex weren't at our usual table. I was walking around, probably looking really confused, when someone called my name.

I turned around and saw Trudie waving frantically in the air. I looked around one last time. Trudie wasn't my first choice of lunch company, but I didn't want to sit alone. I walked over and sat at the end of their group. If people saw me with this group—

Oh, what did I care? My best friends weren't talking to me anymore. I didn't have anything else to lose.

Trudie was about to prove me wrong on that one.

"Avoiding Alex?" she asked as soon as I sat down.

I looked around at each of Trudie's friends. What did they know?

"You know, that whole thing with the note," one of Trudie's friends said. I think her name was Karyn with a *y*.

"Note?" I asked. My heart skipped a beat. What note? Maybe this was about the cards attached to the roses I'd gotten. Those would count as "notes," wouldn't they?

It hit me at the same time Trudie clued me in to what was going on. The note. I'd written a note in homeroom and had given it to Alex.

"You know, that note that said you liked him," Trudie said. "They were passing it around."

"Someone in my third-period gym class had it," one of Trudie's other friends said.

"Why is Alex mad at you?" Trudie asked.

Right. That was what the note had said. It hadn't said anything about me liking him. Where had they gotten that? That was my private note. The one only he was supposed to see. And now the whole school knew about it?

My chest started feeling all panicky, and I reminded myself I had to calm down. I couldn't let them see me like this. They'd tell everyone. I had to at least pretend to be calm and try to fix this.

"He's mad because Ashleigh's mad," I said. It was the truth. "But I never said I liked him."

Karyn with a *y* jumped in. "'I miss hanging out with you,'" she recited in a melodramatic voice.

"'Just us,'" Trudie added. She sounded dramatic too. "Sounds like you like him to me."

"Well, I don't," I said. I knew no matter what I said, they wouldn't believe me. I couldn't believe that the whole school seemed to think I liked Alex.

Including . . . Alex.

I looked around. Had *he* shown others the note? Why? Still no sign of him. Had he and Ashleigh gone somewhere else to avoid all this? To avoid me?

"Excuse me," I said, jumping up.

"Where are you going?" Trudie asked. "You haven't eaten any of your lunch."

"I'm not hungry," I said. "I have to take care of something."

I dumped my lunch into the trash can and rushed off in search of Ashleigh and Alex. They had to be in this school somewhere. Once I found them, I was going to clear everything up, starting with this crazy rumor that I liked him. First, though, I had to know one thing.

Why had he let other people read my note?

CHAPTER FOURTEEN

♥

To: Mia

From: Alex

Best friends don't set each other's crushes up with someone else.

Alex and Ashleigh were good at hiding. But not as good as I was at finding. I didn't know where Ashleigh was, but Alex was eating lunch in the library. He didn't look up until I said his name.

"Hey," he said. He chewed his sandwich while continuing to stare at me. He was waiting for me to say something else. I stomped over to the table and sat down across from him.

"You showed people my note," I said accusingly.

His eyes went wide, and he stopped chewing. He was surprised. As his face scrunched up, I realized that he had no idea what I was talking about.

"I gave you a note in homeroom," I said. "People are talking about it."

"I didn't see any note," he replied. "What did it say?"

At that moment, I knew he was telling the truth. I'd set the note down, but he'd never even looked at it. Was it possible it had somehow slid off his book and someone else had picked it up?

"The note just asked you to please not be mad at me—"

"I'm not mad at you," he said. He shrugged. "Ashleigh is."

"But you didn't talk to me in homeroom," I said. "You wouldn't even look at me, even when I was staring right at you."

Alex set his sandwich down and looked at me. "I don't want to be in the middle of this," he said. "Whatever you and Ashleigh have going on, that's your business. I'm just . . ."

"What?" I asked when he didn't finish his sentence. When he finally did look at me, there was something I hadn't seen in his eyes for a long, long time. He was . . . hurt.

"You could have helped me with the whole Sun thing," he said. "I thought we were better friends than that. I mean, you were trying to match her with someone else, even though you knew I liked her."

Was I really that selfish? Yes, I'd known it had probably bothered him that I was playing matchmaker for Sun and

Kurt, but I thought he'd get over it and go back to being normal.

Go back to being the Alex I knew.

"I don't get it," Alex said. "All you do is worry about everyone else. What happened to the fun girl who used to just hang out?"

It took me a second to realize he was talking about me. Me, the girl who was just wondering the exact same thing about him.

But instead of saying that, I said, "I'm still here. I just wanted to help people. Why is there something wrong with that?"

"We miss you, that's all," Alex said with a shrug.

I smiled. "Well, I'm here. And I have good news."

"What are you doing here?" I heard Ashleigh ask.

I'd been fully prepared to tell Alex everything Sun had said. Minus, of course, the part about me having already talked to Kurt. But before I could get the words out, my best friend's voice interrupted.

I turned around. "Ashleigh," I said. "Listen—"

"She has the whole school thinking you guys are going out now," Ashleigh told Alex. She was looking right past me, as if I weren't even there. "Everyone's talking about it."

"I didn't tell people anything," I said. "I wrote Alex a note, and someone has it."

"You wrote a note saying we were going out?" Alex asked.

"No," I said. "I said I missed *us*."

"What does that mean?" Ashleigh asked. She had that sound in her voice again. The one that said she didn't approve. What was *with* her lately?

"It means that I want things back the way they used to be," I said. "Which was exactly what Alex was just say—"

"You like Alex," Ashleigh said, still looking at Alex. "She likes you. She's liked you for a while."

I spun around. "No, I don't," I said. Then, realizing what I'd said, I turned around to look at Alex. "Not that there would be anything wrong with that or anything."

He just sat there, staring at me, his eyes wide. I knew what he was doing. He was rethinking everything that had happened over the past . . . forever, probably. Analyzing it all as, *She had a crush on me the whole time*, instead of, *She was my BFF who cared about me and would never like me like that.*

He saw my weird behavior with Sun as jealousy now, I just knew it. And I could see how he'd think that. But it wasn't jealousy. Really. It—wasn't. Wasn't . . .

As I stood there, ready to argue my side, I felt all the fight drain out of me. I had no idea why, but I couldn't say that I wasn't jealous. And that was weird.

"Oh, come on," Ashleigh said. "We've all known it for a while. You like him, he likes you. He thought he liked Sun, but he really doesn't. He likes you. Now the whole school knows it. There." She crossed her arms over her chest. "Now that it's all in the open, can we stop trying to fix everyone up with everyone else? Or is that the point."

That last part was said as a statement, not a question. She had a look on her face like she'd just figured out everything. Maybe she had. Maybe she knew more than I did. I was so confused at this point, I didn't know what to think.

I started to deny it. The words were on the tip of my tongue. But then I saw the look on Ashleigh's face. It was the first time she hadn't been mad at me since Saturday. It seemed, for a second, like I almost had my friend back.

I was so relieved, I couldn't deny what she was saying. I didn't know if it was true or not.

Was it true?

It was.

I liked Alex.

The words seemed to echo in my head. I knew I'd have to think about them a little longer. All I knew now was that I missed laughing and smiling with my best friends. Whatever it took to get back to that, I'd do.

Ashleigh's smile widened. She looked like she'd figured it all out, even though I'd said nothing. She wasn't giving me a cold look anymore, but the last thing I wanted was for Alex to think I liked him. Not until I knew for sure he liked me back.

But then Ashleigh said something that wiped the smile right off my face.

"Well, then, I'll just leave you two little lovebirds alone," she said, spinning around and marching out of the library. That left me sitting across from Alex, with an awkward silence between us.

"We aren't lovebirds," I said. I couldn't even look at him while I said it.

"I know," he said. His voice sounded weird.

"Ashleigh should know better," I said. "She's known us for, like, forever, right?"

He nodded. Still, he wasn't making eye contact with me.

"We're friends," I continued. "We'll always be friends. In fact, I came to tell you something. . . ."

He looked up at me, finally making eye contact, and I stalled. What I was supposed to say at that point was that Sun liked him. It was just what he'd wanted to happen. But when I opened my mouth, the words wouldn't come out. In fact, I found I didn't like the thought of Alex liking Sun and Sun liking Alex back.

I was actually jealous.

This was all new to me, and it had me freaked out. I needed time to step back and think. I did that, literally, standing up and backing toward the door.

"What?" Alex asked.

"Nothing." I shook my head. "I—um—have to go."

"But—" Alex stood and started to follow me. He wanted to say something, I could tell, but I couldn't hear it right now. I couldn't hear some long explanation of how he didn't like me that way and he wanted to just be friends. I didn't recognize any of the things I was feeling right now, but I knew they weren't good. They meant I'd gone from just hanging out with my friends and enjoying life to being one of those girls who had one of those things they called a crush.

Yuck.

⌒ᴑᴑᴑ⌒

"Did you talk to him?"

That was the first thing Sun asked me when I arrived at my locker after last period. I'd gotten so caught up in the drama with Ashleigh and Alex, I'd forgotten about Sun's drama.

"Who?" I asked. I stepped up to my locker and opened it. She couldn't be talking about Alex after all everyone had been saying all day.

"Alex," Sun said, proving me wrong. "You said you were going to talk to him."

"You said you wanted me to try to get you together Friday," I pointed out. "At the lock-in."

I gave her a look. She leaned against the locker next to me and stared straight ahead dreamily. I had a feeling she hadn't heard a word I'd said.

"He passed me in the hall earlier," she said. "He didn't even look at me. Do you think he thinks I'm cute?"

I stopped short at that thought. *Alex. Cute.* Instantly an image flashed through my mind. It was an image of Alex sharing his ice cream cone with me the time I'd accidentally dropped mine. That was followed by an image of him smiling at me, that dimple on his left cheek making him look so cute.

"You don't think he thinks I'm cute, do you?" she said.

Wait—what—that's right. She hadn't been reading my mind. She'd been asking . . . asking if I thought Alex thought she was cute. I wasn't going to get away with not answering this.

"I don't know," I said. "You'd have to ask him."

I said that, but the last thing I wanted was for her to ask Alex anything. I knew she wouldn't do that, though. She didn't even have the courage to walk up and introduce herself to him.

"I couldn't do that," she said. "But *you* could. I mean, you guys are good friends, right?"

"Right." I felt a little sick.

"You could ask him if he thinks I'm cute. You don't have to even let him know I like him. Just feel him out and see what he thinks of me first."

"What if he says he doesn't like you?" I asked.

The words were out before I'd really thought them through. It was kind of a rude thing to say, especially since I already knew he thought she was cute. He'd said he liked her. I could just tell her that and she'd be happy. She might even give me the go-ahead to try and get them together. And that was the last thing I wanted.

I was a horrible, horrible person.

"You don't have to do it right this second, either," Sun said. She was gabbing away as we walked down the hall toward the buses. "Just as long as you know something by the time we have the lock-in, it'll be perfect. Then I can try to skate with him or something."

I followed her out of the school. "You can get off at my stop," Sun said as we walked. "I want to show you my wardrobe."

"Your wardrobe?" I asked. I was looking at the bus in front of ours, checking each window for signs of Ashleigh. I realized then I would much rather be hanging out with Ashleigh. I hadn't really realized how much I missed her until then.

"Yes," Sun said. We were at our own bus by then. The driver had already closed the doors and Sun banged on them, while still facing me. "I figure you can help put together a look for Friday night. I want to walk in and have everyone go, 'Wow.'"

She kept talking as we walked down the aisle, making me feel a little nervous. I didn't mind helping people, but it was causing so many problems between me and my friends. Plus, I couldn't help Sun get together with Alex now that I knew I liked him.

We sat behind one of Sun's friends—some girl from math

class. She was hanging on every word we said, and by the time we reached Sun's house, she'd invited herself along. I was worried she'd ask me to help her, too, but I soon came up with an idea. What if I got Sun's friend to learn to help her? Then they could help each other and . . . no need for me, right?

It was the perfect idea. I smiled as we pulled onto Sun's street. I might very well be onto something that could really work.

CHAPTER FIFTEEN

♥

To: Mia
From: Sun
Thanks for changing my life.

"So anyway, we're meeting at my house at six thirty. Don't be late. I heard Kaylee and her girls are planning to dress exactly alike, so let's not do that, right? Ooh, cool boots."

Ashleigh had been talking nonstop since I ran into her at my locker, but something stopped her long diatribe. She was looking off to the right, her gaze focused on the floor. I followed her gaze to a pair of very familiar boots. I'd pulled those same boots from the back of Sun Patterson's closet the previous day and helped pair them with a skirt that looked way too cute for her to walk past Alex. He'd see her and know instantly she was the girl of his dreams. If he didn't know that already.

My first instinct was to run after her and tell her she couldn't wear that, but I had no reason why. All chasing after her would do was upset Ashleigh again anyway.

"Oh, whatever," Ashleigh said, waving her hand in the air.

We started walking in the direction Sun had gone, several feet behind her. I had no idea whether Ashleigh knew it was Sun. She hadn't said. She'd been so busy gawking at Sun's boots, she might not have even seen her face. So far today Ashleigh hadn't gotten mad at me yet, and I hoped to keep it that way.

"Don't you think she's a little dressy for school?" I asked. "I mean, most of us save stuff like that for after school."

"Seriously?" Ashleigh asked, staring at me. "That skirt is key-yoot." That was the word "cute" dragged out. "There are no rules when it comes to looking good."

I was feeling squirmy. The whole thing made no sense. I was the one who had helped Sun look this cute, but I didn't like it. And Ashleigh was the one who had been mad that I was helping other people, and now she was defending one of those people. Then again, she didn't know I'd helped pick this outfit out. I wondered if she'd still think Sun was so cute if she knew I'd helped her yesterday.

I was about to find out.

Sun turned to wave at someone, then saw us out of the corner of her eye. She did a double take, and then a big smile broke out over her face.

"Hi," she said. "What do you think?"

Ashleigh and I both slowed to a stop in front of her. I looked over at Ashleigh to find her expression had changed completely. She gave one of her fake smiles.

"You look great," I said. "We were just saying that. But we have to get to class."

"Wait!" Sun called out as I grabbed Ashleigh's arm and steered her around Sun.

Ashleigh was fine with not stopping, which was fine with me. I sped my footsteps up in the hopes she'd keep up with me.

"Isn't the skirt cute on me?" Sun asked from behind us. That was a safe enough question, but if we stopped, she might bring up something else. Like the fact that I was the one who had recommended these boots with this skirt. "I mean, I know it's kind of fancy for school, but you said yesterday that I had to show it off. I never go anywhere but school."

Uh-oh. I kept walking, but Ashleigh wasn't quite keeping up with me anymore. She'd slowed down.

"What does she mean?" Ashleigh asked.

I turned to see she'd stopped. As I stood there, I weighed my options. I could keep walking and pretend I didn't know Ashleigh was talking to me, but she might be mad at me. I'd just gotten her back on my good side.

"She helped me," Sun said, smiling.

"I helped," I said with a shrug. "I just showed her a few things."

"Wow." Ashleigh looked from me to Sun and back again. She didn't look mad. More curious than anything. "That's really big of you."

"What do you mean?" Sun asked.

I squeezed my eyes closed. I was afraid to hear the answer to that question.

"Just that you guys are in competition for the same guy," Ashleigh said. "I wouldn't think you'd be helping her look *better*. Unless . . ."

No. Stop.

"Ashleigh," I said in a warning voice.

"That's it, isn't it?" Ashleigh said. I had no idea where she was going with this, but I wanted to turn and run away. Instead I was rooted to the spot. "She did this on purpose."

Ashleigh gestured to indicate Sun's skirt. "She made you

wear something that will make everyone stare." She shrugged. "It's a no-brainer. She wants other boys to like you so she can have Alex for herself."

"I did not," I protested. "I told her this was an outfit for nights and weekends."

"I don't go anywhere nights and weekends," Sun reminded me.

"That would change if you and Alex got together," Ashleigh pointed out.

"Wait . . . *you* like Alex?" Sun asked.

Sun's words, said with a tone of clear hurt, got both my and Ashleigh's attention. I stalled. What could I say? I wanted to shout *No!* at the top of my lungs, but I couldn't say that word. I couldn't deny liking Alex, no matter how much I wanted to.

"I—I don't know," I said. And that was the honest truth. I didn't know. I had no idea at all.

"You don't know," Sun said. "What does that even mean?" She looked over at Ashleigh and let out an ironic laugh. "I can't believe this. I trusted her. I trusted you." She turned back to look at me, her eyes wide. "You know what? Forget it. Forget I ever told you anything. I don't believe this."

She stomped off down the hall in the opposite direction from the way we'd been walking. That left me standing there with Ashleigh, an awkward silence between us. I didn't know what to say to her at this point. I was so confused over what had just happened. . . . I needed time to think it all through.

"You don't know?" Ashleigh asked. "What do you mean, you don't know?"

"I don't know," I said. "I don't know anything. I have to get to class."

I backed away from her as she gave me a confused look. Did she even realize what she'd just done? She'd made Sun mad and possibly ruined Alex's chances with her. I was happy about that and was mad at myself, but I was still upset that Ashleigh had done such a mean thing.

It wasn't even that Sun was probably mad at me and would never speak to me again. I mean, that was pretty bad. But worse to me was that my best friend—the girl I'd once planned to go to college with and be friends with forever— had totally been a mean girl. Something I didn't think was possible.

"What's wrong?" Ashleigh asked.

I'd started moving away from her, but she stepped toward

me. She planned to follow me. I had to deal with this now.

"You did that on purpose," I said. "You knew she'd be upset. I just don't understand you anymore."

Ashleigh didn't even protest.

I knew even as I was saying the words that I was sealing my lunchtime fate. I'd be sitting with Trudie and her friends again. If they weren't mad at me too.

CHAPTER SIXTEEN

♥

To: Mia
From: The World
Quit being such a drama queen.

"So, girls . . . how was your day at school?"

There it was, the dreaded question. Dad asked that question more nights than he didn't, so it wasn't like it was a surprise or anything. Tonight I stayed quiet, hoping Kellie would answer so I didn't have to.

"I don't want to talk about it," Kellie said.

So much for that.

"What about you, Mia?" Mom asked. "Are you ready for your big lock-in Friday night?"

The lock-in. I'd almost forgotten about that. I had to spend an entire night locked in a building with Alex and Sun. I wondered if I could pretend to be sick or something to get out of it.

I had a feeling Mom wouldn't let me get away with that.

"I guess," I said. Maybe that would be enough.

"Are you going with Ashleigh?" Mom asked.

It was a reasonable question, since Ashleigh's mother was my regular ride to things like this. But I'd spent lunch with Trudie and hadn't even looked in Ashleigh's direction. I didn't want to talk to her even if she wanted to talk to me. I was pretty sure she didn't.

"I don't think so," I said. The words slipped out before I had a chance to think them through. Mom, of course, latched right onto them.

"You don't think so?" she asked. "What does that mean? You and Ashleigh go everywhere together. Are you mad at each other?"

I flashed Kellie my best *help me* look, to which she responded with a look that said, *You're on your own.*

"No, it's no big deal," I said. "I'll see if I can get someone else to take me."

"I just don't understand," Mom said. "You girls have been like two peas in a pod for as long as I can remember—"

"Carla," Dad said in a warning tone. He took a deep breath and looked at Kellie. "Did you bring that form home for your school trip?"

"Yeah," Kellie said. She pushed herself away from the table and headed for her bedroom. Dad called out that she didn't have to get it right now, and Mom yelled something about her getting back here and finishing her dinner, but Kellie kept going. That was fine by me. Anything that kept them from asking questions about me.

"I've been meaning to talk to you about something," Mom said, turning her attention back toward me. I squirmed a little. The spotlight had been off me for all of seven seconds and already it was back on me again. "I ran into Mrs. Mac-Dowell at the grocery store yesterday afternoon."

"Mrs. MacDowell . . . ," I said, racking my brain. There was no teacher at my school with that last name. I knew someone with that last name, but—

"Her daughter goes to your school," Mom said.

"Sun?" I asked.

"Yes, that's it. Beautiful name. Beautiful girl. Her mom said it's all thanks to you."

"Wow," Dad said. "What does that mean?"

Mom smiled at Dad. "Seems our lovely daughter has been performing makeovers on her classmates."

Dad looked at me. "Is that true?"

"No," I said. I looked at Mom. "It's not really a makeover. I just helped one person."

"You helped her with more than just her clothes and how she looks," Mom said. "Mrs. MacDowell was very specific about that. Apparently, Mia has transformed this girl's entire life by making a few tweaks and just being a good friend to her—the first friend she has had in a while."

I looked from Mom to Dad, realizing something for the first time. My parents were proud of me. Really proud of me. Proud of me the way they were usually proud of Kellie. They'd never given me that look before.

This was the first time in a long, long time that I'd felt like I'd done something really good. It had nothing to do with the rose thing. It was the way I'd helped other people and felt good about myself for doing it.

"All it takes is a little boost and someone to believe in you to give you all the confidence in the world," Dad said. "It's pretty amazing."

I stopped trying to hide my happiness at that statement. He was right. I'd noticed that myself. For a short time, it was the reason I'd kept trying to help people.

"What's amazing?"

Kellie's voice rang out behind me. She'd returned, permission slip in hand, just in time to break up the best conversation I'd ever had with our parents. Both Mom and Dad got up and headed toward the kitchen.

"Nothing," I said. "I just did something at school that's kind of good, but it's nothing like the stuff you get credit for doing every single day."

The words came out sounding not so nice, even though I didn't really mean for them to. Kellie's face fell slightly, and her eyes darkened. I'd upset her. I pushed my chair back to get up before she could start yelling at me.

But she didn't yell. Instead she set the permission slip on the table and sat down in the chair next to me.

"It's been bugging you for a while, I can tell," she said quietly.

"What?" I asked. My hand was still on my plate, and I wondered if I should escape this conversation while I could.

"Do you know how many times I wish I were more like you?" Kellie asked.

The words hung in the air. There was no way Kellie ever wished she were more like me. Why would she?

"You're smart, nice, and you have the most awesome

friends," she said. "I hardly even see my friends, between cheerleading practice and having a boyfriend and all. But you get to have Ashleigh over or go to the mall to shop for clothes. Even when I was your age, I didn't have the kind of friends you do. Real friends. Friends that like you for you, instead of just hanging out with you to be seen with you."

I guess I'd never thought of it that way. But strangely, since the rose thing, I kind of got what she was saying. Nobody wanted to be seen with me or anything, but it did seem like people just wanted to hang out with me because they thought I could help them look prettier or get together with some guy they liked. How had I gone from having really good friends to being surrounded by people who just wanted something from me?

"So what else is up with you?" Kellie asked.

Her words snapped me out of my thoughts. "What do you mean?" I asked.

"You haven't been yourself lately. You've been all quiet and stuff. It's a guy, isn't it?"

Immediately, I felt defensive. "Life isn't all about guys," I snapped. "There are other things."

"See, I knew it," Kellie said. "I know my sister. It's about time you got your first crush. So who is it? Alex?"

I tried to hide my surprise, but I wasn't very good at covering up things like that. I bit the inside of my lip and tried to force my expression to stay as neutral as possible. I had to make sure she couldn't see I was surprised she'd guessed it.

"I could have called it years ago," Kellie said. "You guys are perfect for each other."

Okay, no matter how much I wanted to deny that I liked him, I couldn't stop myself from listening to her.

"He doesn't like me," I said with a shrug. "So it doesn't matter."

"You like him?" Kellie asked.

Oops. I didn't realize I was giving myself away. "I didn't say that," I said.

"You didn't have to. It's all over your face."

I guess I mentioned I wasn't good at covering things up. I knew I could keep denying it, but Kellie had known me all my life. She could see right through me.

"Here's what I've learned about guys," she said, leaning forward. Mom and Dad were cleaning up, but I had a feeling they were trying to listen to our conversation. They couldn't hear her if she whispered. "They either like you or they don't. If they don't, there's nothing you can do."

That was great advice, but I had no idea what to do with it. "He likes someone else," I said.

"Does he know how you feel?"

"I think so," I said with a shrug. "I don't know."

"Well, you have a choice," she said after thinking about my answer for a second. "You can wait for him to decide he doesn't like that other girl anymore, or you can let him know you like him now and let him make the choice."

"Just . . . tell him?" I asked. I knew there was no way I'd ever in a million years just come out and say *I like you* to Alex. I mean, was that something people just came out and said? It seemed a little weird to me.

Besides, Kellie wouldn't understand that I wasn't like her. She could just look at a boy and he'd forget any other girl existed. If I looked at a boy, he'd just wonder if something was stuck between his teeth.

"Sure, why not?" Kellie asked. "What do you have to lose?" She leaned forward again and whispered, "Would you rather waste six months wondering or just know, once and for all?"

The answer to that question should probably have been

that I'd rather know. But that wasn't the real answer. The real answer was that if I knew, once and for all, that Alex didn't like me, what then? Things would probably even be weirder between us.

Things were so much simpler before I knew boys could be cute.

CHAPTER SEVENTEEN

❤

To: Mia
From: Mia
Just tell him!

Someone was watching me. Someone might know about my Valentine's Day trick. That same someone might tell everyone in school what I'd done.

Those were the thoughts going through my mind the next morning, when I was walking the halls of school, looking closely at every person who passed. If anyone as much as glanced in my direction, I wondered if that was the person who was watching me.

Of course, it was probably someone I knew. I realized that, but I wasn't speaking to Sun and Ashleigh anymore, I couldn't ask them if they were the ones sending those notes. All I could do was watch strangers and wonder. . . .

There was someone who might talk to me. One good friend who wasn't mad. We hadn't talked much lately because of . . . things, but I thought we might be able to pick up where we'd left off.

I headed straight for Alex's locker, figuring I'd find him there, digging books out and maybe talking to one of his buddies. Instead he was nowhere in sight.

I searched the area; still no sign. I leaned against his locker as I watched for him. He'd be here any second, I figured, so I might as well stand here and wait. What else did I have to do?

I saw him as he rounded the corner. He was talking to someone—listening, mostly. He looked like he was really interested in what the other person had to say.

The problem was the other person was Sun Patterson.

Sun Patterson, the girl who was mad at me because I hadn't told her I liked Alex too. Alex and Sun were walking side by side, happy as could be, and there I stood in front of his locker like I'd been waiting for him to show up.

Just as I was trying to make myself move, so I could run far, far away, Alex turned and looked right at me. His smile fell. That was all I needed to see. He wasn't happy to see me, so now it was definitely time to *run*.

I don't know if Sun ever saw me or not. All I knew was that Alex saw me, and Alex was with Sun now. They were obviously together, and I wasn't sure I'd ever be able to show my face in front of the two of them again.

Worst of all, I realized as I walked to homeroom, I had to live with this really, really sad feeling that I'd had Alex as a friend for years and now I wouldn't. I already missed him.

"You have to help me with my hair."

I looked up, suddenly realizing someone was talking to me. It was Trudie, and she was staring at me like I was the answer to all her problems. This was my punishment for sitting with them at lunch. Maybe it would have been better if I'd stuck with the original plan to hang out in the library by myself at lunch. I'd only nixed that idea when I imagined Alex and Sun all snuggled up in the reference section.

"I can't do it on my own," Trudie said, pulling on the end of her short ponytail. "As you can see. I've tried deep treatments and every conditioner you can think of—"

"Have you asked a hairstylist?" I asked.

She frowned at me. The look on her face told me she hadn't thought of that. I guess she needed someone to give her a slight shove in the right direction. Maybe if I did that,

I wouldn't have to spend an entire day at the mall with her while she tried on clothes and got her hair done.

"She's trying to impress someone," Karyn said.

Trudie flashed her a hateful look. "Am not," she said.

"Are too," Karyn argued.

I looked from Karyn to Trudie and back again, frowning. I was out of the matchmaking business. I was out of the helping-other-people business too. I just wanted to hang out, eat lunch, and talk about shows I liked and music I'd downloaded, like Ashleigh, Alex, and I used to do.

"I can't help you," I said. "I have no idea what I'm doing."

They were all looking at a spot behind me now, and all of a sudden, I was completely forgotten. I turned around. Now what?

Kaylee was standing directly behind my chair, a hand on each hip.

"Come sit with us," she commanded.

It was an order, not a request. I looked over at Trudie and her friends, all staring straight up at the most popular girl in school with their mouths wide open. I knew that look all too well. It was the same look I'd probably given every time I'd been up close to her since fourth grade.

"Why?" I asked.

"Just do it," Trudie whispered. She leaned closer. "She's Kaylee Hooper."

As *if* Kaylee couldn't hear that. Seriously. She was standing right here. I did my best to act like it was no big deal as I picked up my tray and followed Kaylee back to her table. But I was well aware that everyone in the cafeteria might be watching at that very moment, including Ashleigh.

Ha. Served her right.

"Sit there," Kaylee ordered, pointing to a spot between Rosalia and Makayla.

I set my tray down and pulled the chair back. I knew I was supposed to feel lucky to be asked to sit here, but did Kaylee have to be so rude? I took a deep breath and reminded myself I just had to put up with this for a few minutes and I could go back to Trudie, where I didn't belong either. In fact, it didn't seem like I belonged much of anywhere these days.

"I hear you're a matchmaker," Kaylee said. "They're calling you the miracle worker."

Everyone was staring at me. Were they serious? Miracle worker?

"Look what you did with Squirrel Patterson," Kaylee said. "I mean, *Sun* Patterson."

Everyone giggled. Everyone, that was, but me and Kaylee.

I would have defended Sun, but what was the point?

"Sun isn't speaking to me anymore," I said.

"Why not?" Makayla asked.

I realized as they all turned to look at me that if I said anything more, I'd just be giving them information they'd share with everyone they knew. They didn't care about me. They just wanted to find out what they could get from me.

"Whatever," Kaylee said, pulling the attention back to her. "The point is, you've done a lot with not a lot. If you can do that, you can help me."

Before I could voice the next, obvious question—which was, *What could I possibly do to help someone like you?*—Shonda spoke up. "There's a guy," she said.

Kaylee flashed her a look before turning back to me. "It's a guy you know," she said. "I think he's a good friend of yours."

Not Alex. But it had to be. I didn't have any other guy friends. I didn't even have *that* guy friend anymore, actually, since we hardly talked anymore. That was something I'd point out when she told me she liked Alex. I couldn't help her if he wasn't my BMFF anymore.

"I think I can stop you right there," I said, holding up a hand.

Kaylee blinked in surprise. Nobody stopped her. Nobody held a hand up to dismiss something she was saying. Nobody but me. I was stopping her.

"Alex and I aren't friends anymore," I said. "And besides, I think he's with Sun."

"Really?" Faith asked.

"Who cares?" Kaylee snapped. She narrowed her eyes at me. "I'm talking about Kurt Barnes."

Kurt Barnes? It took me a second to backtrack over our conversation and figure out what she was saying. Wait . . . Kaylee Hooper liked Kurt Barnes?

"He's definitely cute-ified himself lately," Shonda said, nodding and smiling broadly.

"Hey," Kaylee said, glaring at Shonda. "Back off." She turned back to me. "So what do you say?"

"To what?" I asked.

"Have you been paying attention? Me and Kurt," Kaylee snapped. "Make it happen."

I opened my mouth to answer, but the bell rang and people began to scatter. I looked down at my tray. All this and I hadn't even had a chance to eat lunch.

By the time I put my tray up and turned around, Kaylee and her group were gone. Fine by me. I was walking toward the door, my mind trying to process what Kaylee wanted me to do, when I saw Ashleigh and Alex. They were waiting for me near the door.

"You were sitting with Kaylee," Ashleigh said. "Why?"

I came to a stop in front of them. I hadn't prepared for this question, especially since we still weren't speaking. I might have been able to come up with something overnight, once it all made a little more sense to me. So instead of making up some fancy story, I just told the truth.

"She likes someone. She wants me to help."

I shrugged at the end of that and waited for them to speak. They looked at each other, and Alex turned back to me.

"Who?" he asked.

"Nobody important," I said, and that was the truth. Neither one of them had paid a bit of attention to Kurt over the years, so what difference did it make?

"He'll be important once Kaylee gets her hands on him," Ashleigh said. She crossed her arms over her chest. "But I don't get why she needs your help. She's Kaylee Hooper."

"I have no idea," I said.

"Mia helps people," Alex said. "That's what she does now."

I looked at him. It was hard to make eye contact with him now, especially after everything Ashleigh had said about us liking each other. I knew he didn't like me, but just now, when he was staring at me, he had this look like he wanted to say something he would never have the nerve to say.

Of course, I knew he only wanted to say that he missed me as a friend. Something like that. He didn't like me that way. He liked Sun. And now it looked like they were an official couple, so if I wanted to be around Alex at all, I had to suck up whatever feelings I was having and be his friend again. That was how it worked.

"I'm not helping people anymore," I said. Then, realizing how that sounded, I rushed to add to it. "I mean, I'll help people, like if they're hurt or something, but I'm not going to work all that hard to help everyone else. It was upsetting certain people too much."

I looked directly at Ashleigh as I said that last part. Her expression changed then. Softened a little. I knew right then I'd said the right thing. I'd finally gotten through to her. Maybe this was our reconciliation. I hoped so.

Surprisingly, though, Alex was the one who spoke. "She just wants you to spend more time with us," he said. "*We* want you to spend more time with us," he added. "We miss you."

"I miss you guys too," I said. My voice caught a little when I said it.

"I'm sorry," Ashleigh said. "I know I was way out of line with the whole thing with Sun."

"What thing with Sun?" Alex asked.

We'd stopped in front of my locker, and I turned to face them. Ashleigh and I shared a look. The "Sun thing" had been when Ashleigh had told me and Sun that we both liked Alex. I'd assumed Ashleigh had already told Alex about it, but maybe not.

"Nothing," Ashleigh and I said at the same time.

"That's okay," I told Ashleigh, rushing to change the subject. "I'm sorry I've been so weird lately. I got caught up in things, I guess."

"Okay, I'm sorry too," Alex said.

The warning bell rang, and they took off toward their own lockers. I opened my own locker. I was still running the conversation we'd just had over in my head when something fell, smacking me against the forehead before dropping to my feet. Another rose. And it had a card attached.

To: Mia
From: Your Secret Admirer
Soon everyone will know the truth. Get ready for fireworks!

CHAPTER EIGHTEEN

♥

To: Alex
From: Mia
You look really cute tonight.

Kaylee was calling again. I saw the number and quickly pressed a button to silence the phone before Ashleigh heard it. We had thirty minutes until we had to leave Ashleigh's house for the lock-in, and I didn't want to deal with Kaylee right now.

Not that Kaylee and I were BFFs or anything. In fact, I'd pretty much been avoiding her at school. Every time she saw me she asked the same, annoying question.

Have you talked to him yet?

No, I hadn't talked to Kurt. I wasn't going to talk to Kurt. It was none of my business.

"Who was that?" Ashleigh asked, looking at my phone.

"Nobody," I said.

"Can you do my eye makeup?" Ashleigh said, waving me toward her. That was her thing now. She'd assumed I was an expert with hair and makeup, even though I knew nothing about any of it. I walked over to where she sat and did my best, though.

"So, what about you and Alex?" Ashleigh asked as I painted shades of pink and purple on her eyelids. I messed up and rubbed it in, then added more.

"What about us?" I asked.

"What's the update?" she asked.

The odd thing about that question was, Ashleigh had been hanging out with him far more than I had lately. She should know what was going on with Alex more than I did. But I decided to enlighten her, since she didn't seem to know.

"Alex likes Sun now," I said.

Ashleigh's eyes popped open—not a good thing to do when someone is working on your eye shadow. Luckily, I pulled the eye makeup applicator back in time or I might have poked her right in the pupil.

"*No*," she said. She sat up straighter in her seat. "How do you know?"

"I saw them together," I said with a shrug. I didn't want her to know how big a deal this was to me.

"When?" she asked.

I thought back. When was that? "Wednesday?"

I moved the applicator back toward her eye, but she brushed my hand away. "You're telling me Alex Hood is going out with Sun Patterson and nobody told me?"

I stepped back to look at her. "He didn't tell you?"

"Not a word," she said.

No surprise. "Alex doesn't like to talk about stuff like that."

Alex could talk for hours about the latest World of Warcraft, but ask him one question about his thoughts on a girl—even me or Ashleigh—and he'd freeze up like someone had cut his vocal cords. It didn't surprise me at all that Alex hadn't mentioned going out with Sun. Everyone in school would probably know before we would.

"I guess you'll find out soon enough," I said, glancing at the clock next to Ashleigh's bed. "They'll be at the lock-in together."

"We're picking him up," Ashleigh reminded me. "I'm going to ask him."

"Yeah, *that* should go well." I could imagine the conversation now. The two of them, sitting in the backseat with me squished between them. Ashleigh would ask him about Sun, and he would curl up in the corner in a little ball and refuse to talk the rest of the ride there.

"Let me see."

Ashleigh leaned forward to look in the mirror. I couldn't tell right away if she liked what I'd done. Even if she didn't love it, she smiled and said, "Thanks."

By the time Ashleigh's mom announced it was time to go, Ashleigh had wiped all her eye makeup off and redone it. That was fine with me. It gave me a chance to do my own makeup. It would have been silly to spend a lot of time trying to look good, since all I'd be doing was watching Alex and Sun make goo-goo eyes at each other all night, but if I didn't try, Ashleigh would give me a hard time about it. It was just easier to put makeup on and wear my nicest pencil skirt and dress top.

"Look at you," Ashleigh said when she finally stopped staring at herself in the mirror long enough to look at me. "You look awesome."

I was standing in front of the full-length mirror on the back of Ashleigh's closet. I hadn't worn this skirt for months, and the last time, it had hung off the sides of my hips with gaps so big I could have put my hands in them. I'd grown into it since then, and now it fit exactly as it should. Plus, the light-pink blouse I wore brought out the color in my cheeks, giving me a certain glow.

My heart started racing as soon as we made the right turn onto Alex's street. And then I saw him. He looked *so* cute. It hit me as he stepped out onto his front porch, wearing a crisp white button-down shirt and jeans without rips in them. I was so used to seeing him in T-shirts and torn-up jeans, I had to blink to make sure I wasn't seeing things.

"Ooh, he dressed up!" Ashleigh said as he neared the car.

I could feel myself blushing, even though Alex couldn't hear us. In a few seconds he'd be in the car, and there would be that weird silence as Ashleigh and her mom thought about what Ashleigh had just said. So I rushed to keep that from happening.

"He dressed up for Sun," I said. "They're together now."

It still bothered me to say that. I guess I should have been okay with it. I was the one trying to get everyone together, after all. If I hadn't wanted Alex to find a crush, I shouldn't have given him that rose, right?

"Then why isn't he going to the lock-in with her?" Ashleigh asked.

I bit my lip. Good question. Liking boys was *so* confusing. Alex climbed into the car on my side. Once I saw him reaching for the door handle, I quickly unbuckled my seat belt and started sliding across the backseat. He was watching by then, though, so I was super nervous as I scooted over.

I don't like him. I don't like him. I don't like him.

I kept chanting those three words as Alex fastened his seat belt. Ashleigh's mom started making small talk about silly things. "You excited about tonight? Is everyone going to be dressed up? Will there be food at the lock-in?" Meanwhile, I was staring out the window, my hands clenched in my lap. If I thought hard enough, I was sure I could go back to just being Alex's friend and nothing more.

"Wow," Ashleigh said as we pulled into the parking lot of the city's only family Sportsplex, which was just a few blocks from Alex's house. A big sign advertised ice-skating, bowling, basketball, and swimming. There was a line going all the way back to the street, where people were dropping kids off.

"We can get out here," Alex said.

"Yeah, let's walk," Ashleigh agreed.

Alex was staring at me. I could see it out of the corner of my eye. I looked over at him.

"You up for walking?" he asked.

He was asking just me? For a long second, I felt good about that.

Then Ashleigh spoke up, spoiling the moment. "Let's go," she said. "We can walk it."

Alex took off after her, leaving me no choice but to hurry to catch up with the two of them. I couldn't believe how silly I'd been. Of course Alex wasn't talking to just me about doing something romantic. They just wanted to walk toward the door rather than sitting in traffic for the next ten minutes.

I didn't like this. Not at all. I thought back to the last day of the chocolate rose sale, how I'd just wanted to be more like Kellie and Kaylee. I wanted people to look at me and think I mattered. But now, remembering what it was like to be invisible and ignored, I realized I wanted that back. I wanted to just hang out with my friends and have fun without all this other stuff.

I caught up with Ashleigh and Alex around the time they reached the rest of the crowd. Everyone was trying to push through the four front doors to the place at once. I ended up next to Alex, with the crowd pushing us up against each other. I couldn't even look at him as our arms smushed together.

"Mia!" I heard someone call as we passed through the door and came out into the huge lobby.

"Hi, Kaylee," Ashleigh said.

Ignoring Ashleigh, Kaylee looked at me. "Come here."

No, I hadn't talked to him yet. She wouldn't like that answer. The only answer she wanted to hear was that I'd talked to Kurt and he knew she liked him. Oh, and that he liked her, too.

"Go," Ashleigh whispered, giving me a big nudge in the arm. When I didn't go, she actually gave me a little shove in Kaylee's direction.

Great. Now there was no way to avoid talking to her.

It would have been easier for me just to tell Kurt that Kaylee liked him. I knew that. But every time I started to walk over to Kurt and tell him she liked him, something stopped me. I guess part of me still hoped Sun and Kurt would get together, leaving Alex single. But I knew that was wrong of me, so I didn't really admit it to myself.

"Did you talk to Kurt?" Kaylee asked for what must have been the millionth time that week.

I shook my head. "I didn't get a chance," I said. Which was true, I guess. Truer than saying I tried to talk to him or I almost talked to him. I backed away, moving toward my friends, to send the clear message that I didn't want to stand here and talk about this.

But Kaylee's face had changed. Her eyes had darkened

and her entire expression was . . . angry. Uh-oh. This was a girl who always got her way.

"You said you would," she said. "You said you would before tonight."

Her voice grew louder with each word she spoke. I looked around nervously, worried about who might be able to hear. The answer to that was, *everyone*. There were so many people around, our conversation could pretty much be overheard by the entire seventh grade at that point.

"I'll talk to him," I whispered, holding my hands up to calm her down.

"Forget it," she said in a huff. "I'll do it myself." She looked around and took off down the hall, her friends chasing after her.

I shrugged as I turned back toward my friends. They were standing right behind me, waiting.

"I don't know why she didn't do that in the first place," I said, shaking my head. "It's not like she's shy."

"She wants you to talk to Kurt?" Ashleigh asked, a strange look on her face.

"Yeah," I said. What was going on here? Ashleigh looked like she knew something.

"She was doing it on purpose," Ashleigh said. "She knows I like him."

Wait. *Say what?*

I had about a billion questions I wanted to ask, but Ashleigh started toward the basketball courts, where everyone else was going. Signs pointed in that direction, so everyone just followed them.

"She likes Kurt?" I whispered to Alex as we walked, side by side, along with the crowd.

"Yes," he said. I realized I was leaning close enough to him to whisper. It made me all butterfly-ish in my stomach.

"But what about Rob?" I asked. "She's liked him forever."

Alex shrugged.

"She didn't tell me," I said.

"Well, you guys haven't been talking much," he said.

He was right. I hadn't talked to her about liking Alex, either. Even after she'd brought it up, we still weren't really talking about it. How could I expect her to talk to me about her crush if I wasn't talking to her about mine?

But Kurt Barnes? Really? I would not have guessed that.

"But wait—" I reached out and grabbed Alex's arm. He stopped. People moved around us, but I didn't pay any attention to them. "Why would that make Kaylee like him too?"

Alex sighed. "It's fun for her. The whole 'get Ashleigh's

best friend to fix us up' thing is a challenge. Come on. We'd better go if we want pizza."

I followed him into the room, feeling a little numb as my mind tried to process all this new information. Ashleigh and Kurt. Kurt and Sun. Kurt and Kaylee.

"So that's why you were so mad," I said when I caught up to Ashleigh. She was at the end of the pizza line, waiting for us. Alex stepped up next to her and turned to look at me. I guess he was expecting this.

"Huh?" Ashleigh asked.

"When I was trying to fix Sun up with Kurt, you got really mad," I said. "I didn't know why. I thought it was because I wasn't getting Alex and Sun together. It was really because you liked Kurt too."

Ashleigh finally realized what I was saying. She stopped looking around to see who else she could talk to and actually looked at me. I thought about bringing up the fact that she could have told me she liked Kurt, but she really couldn't. I was too busy trying to get Kurt together with everyone else in school.

"I'm sorry," I said. "I didn't know. I thought you still liked Rob."

"Well, now you know," she said. There was a hint of

sadness in her voice, and I couldn't believe I'd been such a bad friend. I thought back to all the things I had done to help Sun, as well as what Kaylee had been trying to get me to do.

"She didn't know," Alex said to Ashleigh. He looked over at me. "You didn't know. You couldn't have known."

"Not unless Ashleigh had told me." I looked over at Ashleigh after I said that. See how I'd turned it around on her? Not to be mean or anything, but it felt good to be the good guy for once. It also felt good to know why she had been mad at me. That would help me never do it again.

Ashleigh looked sad for a second, lowering her gaze toward the ground. Just when I thought I might have to cheer her up again, that gaze of hers suddenly fled to something behind me. Her eyes widened.

"He's behind you," she whispered.

"Who?" I asked, starting to turn around.

She reached out and grasped my forearm so hard, it hurt. "Don't look," she urged, still in a whisper.

"Kurt," Alex said. He looked bored with the whole thing.

"He can wait in line with us," I said, turning to wave him over. The line for pizza was long, so people probably would be mad if I let Kurt break the line. I didn't care, though, if it meant I could help Ashleigh and Kurt get to know each other.

"No!" Ashleigh said. This wasn't whispered, but at least she wasn't grabbing my arm and practically breaking it again.

"I can help you two get to know each other," I said, but this time I didn't turn around. "Isn't that the whole point?"

"She likes to help people," Alex said. "She wants to help you."

"I want to help you," I repeated. I hated to sound like a copycat, but this was big. I'd spent so much time helping all these other people that now I just wanted to help my BFF.

"Not with me around," Ashleigh whispered. "Besides . . . Kaylee."

I shook my head. "Don't worry about Kaylee. She doesn't stand a chance with him. She may be able to boss the rest of us around, but she can't boss a boy into liking her. It doesn't work that way—"

No telling how long I would have continued on my tirade if Alex hadn't spoken up to stop me. "No," he said. "Kaylee. Behind you."

I turned around, and sure enough, Kaylee was with Kurt, blinking her eyes and smiling slyly up at him. She was doing exactly what she'd said in the hallway. Of course she didn't need me to talk to Kurt for her. I was just that extra kick. What better way to make Ashleigh more upset than having her BFF do the setup?

"See?" Ashleigh asked. "That's what happens when Kaylee finds out I like someone."

I looked at Alex. This was what they'd been talking about. So it was true. Kaylee was doing this on purpose.

"She overheard me talking to Alex," Ashleigh rushed to explain, probably noticing the confused expression on my face. "It was during the time you and I weren't talking, or I would have told you, too."

We weren't speaking for, like, a minute. Even if that happened to be the minute she'd decided to pour her heart out about her feelings for Kurt, why would she tell Alex, of all people? He'd tell her to get over it and punch her in the arm or something.

"It turns out, Alex is a great listener," Ashleigh said. "Almost as good as you. He didn't try to talk me out of it or anything. But Kaylee did."

"Kaylee did what?" I asked. I was still a little surprised that Alex had been a great listener. He always was a great listener when I talked about my problems, but he was weird about the whole boy-girl thing. If I'd told him I had a crush on Kurt, for instance, he would have blushed and changed the subject—

Wait. Maybe that wasn't because he didn't like to talk

about stuff like that. Maybe he just didn't like talking about stuff like that with *me*.

"Kaylee tried to talk her out of it," Alex said. "She was standing right behind us in line at the Dairy Dip when we were talking about it."

"I didn't think anyone from school would be there," Ashleigh said. She shrugged and gave a half smile. "Surprise, I guess, right?"

I turned to look at Kaylee. The part of me that protected my best friend at all costs wanted to go yell at her or something, but I knew that would only make the whole school talk about me on Monday. Funny, since that was what I thought I wanted. Now I was tired of being talked about.

"She's coming this way," Ashleigh whispered. She looked down, shielding her face with her hand, as if that would keep Kaylee from seeing her.

I wasn't afraid to face her. I spun around and looked directly at her, putting on my bravest expression.

"There," Kaylee said. She came to a stop in front of me, a smug smile on her face. Claire and Shonda stood right behind her, mimicking her stance. No telling where the other five of her groupies had gone. "That's how it's done."

"How what is done?" I asked, and, if I must say so myself, it was a pretty darn good acting job.

"*That* is how a girl gets a boy she likes," Kaylee said. Her arms were crossed over her chest, and she looked me up and down with a condescending expression on her face. "If someone really has confidence, she doesn't have to wait around for Cupid here to take care of things for her."

I could have pointed out that if she really had confidence, she would have done that days ago. But it was time to end this matchmaking stuff once and for all.

I shrugged. "You're right."

I'm sure I looked just as surprised as I felt that those words came out. At least it wiped that smirk off Kaylee's face.

"What's that supposed to mean?" she asked.

I shrugged. "Just that you're right. Everyone should have the courage to walk up to the boy she likes and just say so."

"But we don't," a girl's voice behind me said. It wasn't Ashleigh's. The voice belonged to Sun. I turned around and saw Sun and Gillianni standing there . . . together.

My gaze automatically flew to Alex, who wasn't looking at Sun, even though she stood next to him. No surprise. He was probably too shy to look her way.

"We don't have the nerve to do something like that," Sun

said. I looked from her to Gillianni. Were they friends now? Sun continued, "That's why we need help."

"She's right," Alex said. "I've liked someone for a while . . . and there's no way I could tell her to her face."

Sun looked at me. I took that look to say, *I'm sorry he likes me instead of you.* The look bugged me, but I had to be a gracious loser. It was the right thing to do.

"That's funny," Kaylee said.

We all turned to look at her. She'd been quiet, briefly, and I was surprised she was still standing there. She had, after all, gone a full fifteen seconds without being the center of attention.

"What?" Ashleigh asked.

Kaylee sneered again as she spoke. "Alex couldn't tell the girl he liked that he liked her, but he couldn't get Mia to tell her either."

Kaylee snorted. On anyone else it would sound disgusting, but Kaylee made it cute somehow. Even when I didn't like how she'd treated Ashleigh, I couldn't help but think that.

"What are you talking about?" Ashleigh asked. She didn't ask it nicely, either.

"I'll be right back," Alex said, whipping around and rushing off. We all watched him go. What was up with him?

"Oh, please," Kaylee said. "I don't have time for this. Everyone knows Alex likes Mia and has for a bazillion years. That's not the point. The point is . . ."

I didn't hear anything else Kaylee said. Everyone knew Alex liked me? And he had for a bazillion years?

Alex liked me?

It couldn't be true. If it was true, I would have known something by now, wouldn't I? He'd always thought of me as a friend and only a friend.

"Gotta go," Kaylee said. "Kurt's waiting for me. Toodles."

She spun around in her furry boots and sauntered off, Claire and Shonda trailing after her. I turned back to Ashleigh and pounced.

"What was she talking about?" I asked. Because if something was going on with Alex I needed to know about, Ashleigh would know. She'd spent a lot of time around him lately.

"He has been kind of down in the dumps," Ashleigh said. "I thought it was because he missed you. I guess it's because he . . . *missed you*."

As little sense as that probably made to Sun and Gillianni, it made total sense to me. I looked at the two of them and saw them toss each other a glance before facing me again.

"People kind of knew that," Gillianni said.

I looked at Sun. People may have known that, but no way did she.

"I knew," Sun said, probably noticing my confused expression. "That's why I was so upset when I found out you liked him, too. Don't worry, I didn't tell him."

"But . . . I saw the two of you together." My mind was actually replaying the image of the two of them talking in the hallway. They'd been all huddled together like they were sharing a secret, romantic moment. . . .

Or just a secret.

"We were talking about you," Sun said. "I asked him if he liked you. He didn't say anything at first. Then finally he admitted it."

"What did he say?" I asked.

"Just one word," Sun said. "Yes."

"You have to go talk to him," Ashleigh said. "I'll get some pizza for all of us."

"One whole pizza for all of us," Sun announced, smiling broadly.

Weird, but that didn't seem to bother Ashleigh. I looked back over my shoulder as I was walking away and saw the three of them create a little circle as they started talking.

Maybe there was hope for Ashleigh and Sun's friendship after all.

As for me, I had to talk to Alex. And I'd never been more terrified in my life.

He was sitting on the front steps of the Sportsplex, in the cold, without a coat. He had to have been freezing, but he didn't show it. Which told me he was that desperate to get away from me.

I stepped tentatively forward. I wasn't really worried he was mad at me or anything. I was just a little embarrassed and a *lot* scared. But I walked toward him anyway, my heart seeming to pound harder with each step I took.

"Hi," I said, mostly so he wouldn't be scared when I got to him.

I scared him anyway. He spun around, looking up at me with wide eyes. In those few seconds, everything I'd thought I was going to say flew straight out of my brain. I was left standing there, staring at him with my mouth open.

Real cool, Hartley, that little voice in my head said. I wouldn't be surprised if he stood up and ran off right at that very second and never spoke to me again.

"Hi," he said. He turned back around. Before he did, I

could have sworn I saw his face turn light pink, like it did whenever he was embarrassed.

"I'm supposed to talk to you," I said. "Ashleigh's saving us some pizza," I added lamely.

That wasn't what I was supposed to talk to him about at all. I gulped against the large lump that had suddenly formed in my throat. When had this happened? I used to be able to talk to Alex without any trouble. Now all this silly "romance" stuff was getting in the way.

He had his elbows propped on his thighs and was staring down at the ground. I took a deep breath and somehow found the courage to keep moving forward. I sat down next to him and looked over at him. He didn't look up.

"Sun likes you," I said. It was the right thing to do, even if it might make him change his mind about liking me. "She wanted me to help you two get together. I didn't want to."

Did I have to say any more than that? I figured that said it all.

"Why?" he asked.

Okay, so I did have to say more. I didn't have the nerve to say anything else, though. I bit my lip and stared down at the ground. Maybe if I focused on the sidewalk long enough, the words would just fall out or something.

"Because . . . you know," I said.

That should have been enough. The old Alex would have let it rest at that. But this Alex didn't let me off that easily.

"No," he said. "I don't."

"I was jealous." There. I'd said it. He wouldn't push any further. I took a deep breath and realized I actually felt relieved that it was all out in the open.

"As a friend or as a . . . you know?" he asked. Now he was the one having a hard time getting things out.

"As a 'you know,'" I said. I finally found the guts to look over at him and smile. "I *like* like you, okay? As more than a friend."

It was probably the hardest thing I'd ever said, but once it was out there I felt much, *much* better. It was this thing that had been hanging in the air between us, but now it was out in the open. Sun had said Alex liked me, too, but I couldn't know for sure unless I heard him say the words.

He looked up at me and smiled. And then he stood up and held out his hand, waiting for me to put my hand inside it. Hand in hand, we walked into the Sportsplex together.

CHAPTER NINETEEN

❤

To: Mia
From: You Know Who
You can only keep secrets for so long before they all come out.

I'm not sure what I expected when we returned, but I know what I *wasn't* expecting, and that was exactly what I saw as soon as we walked through the door to the basketball court.

People were everywhere, gathered in groups on the floor as they happily munched on pizzas. The committee had decided to do this picnic-style. I spotted Sun's arm up in the air as she waved frantically to us, but she was sitting with only Gillianni.

Where was Ashleigh?

I got my answer as I followed Alex across the court.

We wove through the groups of people, and my stomach growled. I realized I was starving.

We were almost to Sun and Gillianni when I spotted Ashleigh. And Kaylee. And Kaylee's entire entourage. And in the center of all that was Kurt Barnes.

I nearly tripped over my own feet looking over at Kurt's face. He did not look happy. In fact, my eyes made contact with his, and I noticed his expression seemed to scream one thing.

Help me.

Weird. I would think most boys would love being surrounded by pretty girls, but Kurt looked completely freaked out by it. Probably because of the way they were all talking to him at once. Loudly. I waved to Ashleigh to come with me, but she was staring at Kurt so intently, I guess she didn't notice.

Sun was beaming up at us when we returned. She had that proud mama look, which made me feel better. I'd been worried she wouldn't want to be my friend anymore if I was with Alex.

"Ashleigh's doing her best, but I'm not sure she can beat Kaylee," Gillianni commented.

We all turned and looked at the silliness taking place just

a few feet away. Sure enough, Kaylee had shoved her way in front of Kurt and was being her usual charming self, while Ashleigh sat off to the side, ignored.

She looked over at us and, all at once, the four of us motioned for her to come over. Why would she want to sit over there being ignored when she could come hang with us?

Nobody seemed to notice as Ashleigh rose to her feet and started toward us. Even more reason for her to leave.

"Forget him," Sun said as Ashleigh plopped down, looking miserable. "He's not worth it."

"I know," Ashleigh said. "I don't really like him all that much anymore. He's kind of dull. I just hate for Kaylee to win."

"I don't think she *is* winning," Sun commented.

We all turned around. Kurt stood up, a slice of pizza in one hand and his bottle of water in the other, and walked away. That left Kaylee staring up at him, her mouth hanging open.

"Fail!" Alex said, loudly enough that it made me nervous. What if Kaylee overheard and marched over here to tell him off? But if she heard, she didn't respond. She just shrugged and turned back to her friends, who leaned forward to console her.

"Give me a break," Gillianni said around a mouthful

of pizza. "They act like Kaylee's the first person to ever be rejected."

"Not the first person," I said. "But it's probably the first time in her life anybody ever said no."

"He didn't even do that," Alex said. "He just got up and walked off. Total burn."

I turned and looked at Kaylee again. She was totally acting like nothing had happened, but I knew she was embarrassed. I didn't think anyone was paying attention but us, but she was leaning in toward her friends like she didn't want anyone to look at her.

"Kurt said no to her," Ashleigh said.

We all turned to look at her. How would she know that? She'd left before he got up.

"He was telling us he was too busy to go out with anyone," Ashleigh said. "But Kaylee kept pushing and pushing. He looked like he wanted to run when I was sitting there. That's why I was glad when you guys waved me over. I was just hanging out because I thought he might like me, but obviously, he likes no one right now. He just didn't want to be mean to Kaylee when she walked up to him. If he doesn't want to talk to me, I don't want to talk to him."

I nodded. That was a great attitude to have. As I looked over at Sun and Gillianni, I could see them running that through their thoughts. Good. Maybe it would help them, too.

"So I guess Mia's time as Stanton Middle School's match-maker has come to an end," Ashleigh said dramatically.

"It's about time," I said. "That's a lot of pressure."

"Speaking of pressure," Alex said, nodding at something behind me. I turned to see Kaylee bearing down on us. Her gaze was directed at me.

As I braced myself for her to yell at me, I realized she didn't really look angry. She had that sneer again. The sneer was worse than anger. It scared me.

"So," she said as she stopped just in front of me. "Looks like your little game didn't work."

"What game?" Ashleigh asked, because I didn't have the nerve to. I didn't want to hear whatever she was about to say. I didn't have a good feeling about this.

"That whole rose thing," Kaylee said. "I'll bet you think nobody knew, but I figured it out."

It felt like the entire world around us had gone into slow motion. All I could do was stare up at her, speechless.

"You figured it out," I repeated.

"You know, Kaylee, nobody asked you," Gillianni said. She'd risen up on her knees and was staring Kaylee down, a hand on each hip.

"Nobody asked me, you're right," Kaylee said. "But they should have asked me. In fact, the rest of you should have put it all together by now."

"Put what together?" Sun asked. She was on her knees as well. I had my own little team behind me. Of course, Kaylee's group of friends was even larger.

"The rose thing," Kaylee said. "All that silly froufrou language." She looked around and sighed. "Didn't you think it was weird that they were all signed by a secret admirer?"

"Everyone signs cards as secret admirer," Ashleigh said. "What's your point?"

"Fine. I'll show you." Kaylee reached into her back pocket and held up a piece of paper. I would know that piece of paper anywhere. It was a copy of one of the lists Ashleigh and I had used to take down notes for cards when we sold Valentine's Day roses. That list had been given to the office for their records. I didn't think a student could get a copy of it. I figured Kaylee had found it while in the principal's office, making announcements.

Without giving any of us a chance to respond, Kaylee

tossed the piece of paper toward us. It landed on the floor in front of Ashleigh.

"I hate to ruin the pizza party by giving your little secret away," Kaylee said, but it was obvious she was loving every minute of this. She looked at my friends behind me. "Mia bought a bunch of roses to help us win, then put the names of losers on the list. The committee wrote those names on the cards, and those losers got roses when they wouldn't have normally. This proves all your roses were fake. Read the list if you don't believe me. It's all right there at the bottom in the same handwriting. And it's all the people who shouldn't have gotten roses."

Ashleigh had already picked the list up, and now she looked down at it. "This doesn't prove anything," she said.

"Everything on that list is in the same handwriting with the same dorky wording," Kaylee said. "Some are even written exactly like the others. Not very original, but I guess everyone can't be Shakespeare. Did you get the roses I put in your locker?"

I widened my eyes. "That was you?" I asked.

Kaylee smiled at my friends. "I put some roses in Mia's locker to let her know I'd seen that list she'd made. I saw her turn it into the office Valentine's Day morning and knew she added all those names. I wanted her to know she wasn't getting away with it."

"Wait a second," Alex spoke up to say. "You're telling me that Mia cheated? She's the reason we had a lock-in?"

"I was trying to help everyone," I said. "I wanted us to win the lock-in, but mostly I wanted you guys to get roses. I know how much it sucks to sit there every year, while people like Kaylee get a billion roses and we get none."

Silence. All around us was noise, but the small group gathered around us was dead quiet. I looked at Ashleigh to see if she was mad at me, but mostly she just looked confused. I couldn't blame her. I felt pretty confused myself.

"I think it's great," Sun suddenly said. I turned around and saw her facing off with Kaylee. "She did it to help people."

"So . . . wait," Gillianni said. "Nobody sent me a rose?"

"Mia sent you a rose," Kaylee said. "That's what I'm saying."

She rolled her eyes. We were too dense to keep up with her brain, I was sure she was thinking.

"I don't have a secret admirer," Gillianni said. This time it was more of a statement than a question.

"But look how much confidence you have," I said. "I'm sure you do have a secret admirer by now. That's why I did it."

"See?" Kaylee said. Hadn't she gone away already? "Without Mia's *generous* help, you'd all still be big losers. Aren't you so lucky she took pity on you?"

Her point was clear. They should be mad at me because I thought they needed my help in the first place. It was an insult to all of them.

"That's not how I felt at all," I said. I looked around, desperate for my friends to believe me. None of them were looking at me. "I just wanted to make everyone a little happier. We're all tired of Kaylee getting all the roses every year."

After a long silence, Alex finally spoke up. "So the rose you gave me. That was really from you?"

"Not because she liked you, though," Ashleigh said. There was no missing the little edge to her voice. It said she was mad with a capital *M*. "Because she felt sorry for you."

"That's not it at all," I said. I glanced at Sun. She was the only one who might stand up for me. But even she seemed to be avoiding looking at me. "I liked the fact that you guys were so happy to get roses. It made me feel good."

"You should have just left it like it was," Ashleigh said. She held up the list. "It's better to get no rose than to get a rose from someone who feels sorry for you. I'm going skating. Anyone else?"

Gillianni stood up and trailed after her. Sun stared at Kaylee for a second, then glanced at me, before finally rushing off after them.

I turned to look at Alex. He was staring up at Kaylee, who still hadn't moved. I just wanted her to go away.

"Could you excuse us for a minute?" I asked Kaylee.

She gave me that same self-satisfied smirk before turning and marching off. The message was clear. She'd done her damage. Now it was time to enjoy her pizza.

With her finally gone, I turned around to face Alex. He couldn't be mad at me. We'd just decided we liked each other.

"I was just trying to help," I said. "I wanted you guys to be happy."

He stared at me for a long moment. If he'd stared at me for that long a few minutes ago, I probably would have been all jittery, but now I didn't feel jittery at all. All I knew was I wanted him to say he wasn't mad at me. He understood. He thought it was great what I'd done.

Instead, when he finally spoke, he asked, "Why didn't you send me a rose from you?"

"Because . . ."

I stalled. What answer did I have for that? I hadn't thought of Alex that way until recently. Or maybe I had thought of him that way and didn't realize it. But either way, I couldn't explain it to him.

Instead I said, "I thought we were friends." Then, after thinking about it a second, I added, "You didn't send me a rose either. As friends, we should have been sending each other roses anyway."

That was a very good point, if I had to say so myself. But he just looked confused.

"The rose you wrote for me read that I didn't know how great I was," Alex said. "Did you mean that?"

I didn't have to think about that one long. "I did," I said. "And I think after you got the rose, you had a little more self-confidence too."

His face had brightened a little, but now that brightness dimmed. He frowned at me, his eyes narrowed.

"What did the rest of the cards say?" he asked.

He picked the list up. I wanted to reach out and grab it, but I knew that would never go over.

He scanned the list, his frown deepening. I knew what he was reading. It wasn't good.

"I'm not a very good writer," I said. "I had to reuse a few of them. But I meant the words when I wrote them for you."

I knew before he looked up from the list that he wouldn't

be happy about it. I'd written that part about not knowing how great you are for at least eight or nine cards that I could think of. It was a great line—short, sweet, and to the point. But if you were one of the ones who received that card and it was written by the girl you liked, that wouldn't matter.

"This one went to Kurt," he said, frowning as he held up a card that had the same message as his had. Then he added, as if I didn't know, "Kurt Barnes."

"I didn't know him then," I said. "And you and I were just friends . . . I thought."

He lowered the card and looked at me. I could tell he was hurt.

"I liked you," he said. "For a long time, I liked you."

"I didn't know," I said, my voice barely above a whisper. Really, I'd had no idea. How could I have known if he'd never told me?

But as he stepped away to start toward the ice rink, I knew what the answer to that would be. I should have known. He'd given me every chance to know. I just hadn't paid attention.

And now it was too late.

CHAPTER TWENTY

♥

To: Stanton Middle School

From: Mia

Sometimes just saying you're sorry isn't enough.

I was skating alone.

I know, it was silly. I could have sat in the bleachers all alone and watched, but that would just show Kaylee she'd won. So I laced up my ice skates and joined everyone out on the ice.

Every time Kaylee skated by, she giggled and whispered to her friends, so I quickly learned to stop looking her way. I just stared down at my feet to make sure I didn't trip and pretended I was the only one out there.

I was really wishing I'd just let this Valentine's Day be boring and lame after all. All I'd ever wanted was to be popular, yet here I was, the number-one enemy at the lock-in. At least before I'd had friends.

One thing that did happen on my seventh time around the ice was that I accidentally saw Alex and Ashleigh. They were skating side by side, both looking very serious as they talked about something. They looked like they were arguing. About me?

Probably not. I skated past them and kept looking down. I guess I felt like if I looked down, they couldn't see me. At the very least, I wouldn't have to think about them watching me, so that worked. For now, anyway.

"Lump on the ice. Watch out!"

Those words, followed by a round of laughs, brought my attention back to the rink in front of me. The first thing I noticed were people swerving around something on the ice. The second thing I noticed was the lump on the ice.

It was a well-dressed lump with long, beautiful hair. I knew that lump. That lump was Gillianni.

Nobody was around her, not even Sun or Ashleigh. I slowed to a stop near her and looked around. Where were all her friends when she needed them?

It wasn't as bad as I'd thought. Ashleigh and Alex were

coming toward us, a look of surprise on their faces. They'd stop when they got closer, I just knew it. But in the meantime, I had to do something. Kaylee and her friends were still laughing, even though they'd passed her a full minute ago.

"Take my hand," I said, reaching it out to her.

She looked up to me, and I had one of those weird moments. My mind flashed back to five years ago at a completely different skating rink—a regular roller rink. Gillianni had done far more than help me up. She'd stood up for me. So when she reached up and took my hand, flashing me a grateful smile, I knew I had to do more.

I turned around and looked past Ashleigh and Alex, who slid to a stop in front of Gillianni. Sun and Kurt, skating next to each other, were next. I glanced at them briefly, trying to figure out what was going on there, before the sight of Kaylee in my peripheral vision caused me to look past them to her.

Kaylee was no longer smiling. She was staring at Sun and Kurt, who weren't holding hands or anything but were skating alone . . . together. His friends weren't even skating with them. Definitely a reason for Kaylee to be mad, but I'd think about that later.

"Are you okay?" I heard Sun ask as she skated to a stop. Kurt kept going, which wasn't very nice of him, but I didn't have time to worry about that now. I was busy watching Kaylee approach.

"What are you looking at?" Kaylee snapped when she turned her attention from Sun to me. She leveled those beady eyes at me and turned her right foot in front of her to stop.

Apparently, her friends didn't get the message she was about to do that. Christina started it. She slid past Kaylee and, realizing too late what was going on, began waving her hands in the air to try to stop herself. It was no use.

Faith was even less prepared. She slammed right into Kaylee, who fell forward, plunging straight toward the ice. Faith fell soon after, which knocked Ella to the ground, who bumped into Shonda, knocking her down as well.

It would have been funny, if not for the fact that someone really could have gotten hurt. Everyone who had been gathered around Gillianni only seconds ago now rushed forward to help Kaylee and her friends.

"I'm fine, I'm fine," Kaylee snapped as I reached my hand out for her to grasp. She pushed herself up on her knees, then tried to stand, but her skate slipped on the ice and she fell down again. Still, she wouldn't let me help, so I moved over to help Faith, who was a lot nicer about it.

I could tell Kaylee was embarrassed, and despite everything, I kind of felt bad for her. I'd been embarrassed like that myself. Back in second grade, Kaylee had been the cause of my fall, plus she had laughed at me after I fell. This was my chance to get even and laugh at her or skate off and leave her there, but I didn't.

I guess that was the big difference between us.

"Move!" someone shouted, calling my attention to the fact that we were all standing there in a big clump. All of us but Kaylee, who couldn't seem to find her way to her feet. She was even snapping at her friends who were trying to help her.

As I stood back and watched, I realized she was making a fool of herself. Everyone in the rink was staring at her by now and she looked ridiculous, sliding around on the ice, yelling at everyone. The yelling made her look worse than being on the ground. If she'd fallen and looked sad, you'd feel sorry for her, but the yelling just made you wonder what was wrong with her.

"Let's go," Ashleigh said, waving for everyone to follow. Everyone did. None of them looked back at me either.

I trailed along after them as they ignored me. Everyone was still mad at me, I could tell, even though I'd helped Gillianni. I frowned as I skated alone. Apparently it wasn't enough to be nice to people. I had to find a way to make all this up to them.

By the time I came back around, Kaylee was gone. Her friends were gone too. And I had an idea that just might work.

CHAPTER TWENTY-ONE

♥

To: Mia

From: Mia

You're perfect just the way you are.

"What's this?"

I smiled down at Kaylee, who was sneering up at me. Six of her friends were gathered around her, but I started with Kaylee. I set her rose on the desk in front of her and stepped back. Then I started handing roses out to everyone around her.

"Now, you'll notice there's a card attached to each rose," Ms. Phillips, Kaylee's homeroom teacher, announced. It was the following Monday and Ms. Phillips was helping me with my secret plan. "Write the name of the person you want it to go to and write a short message on the card, then hand it back to Mia, who will kindly make sure your rose gets to that person."

"Do we have to pay for it?" someone asked from the back of the room. I didn't look to see who it was. Alex and Ashleigh were back there, and I didn't want to take the chance of making eye contact and losing my nerve completely.

"No, you don't," Ms. Phillips said. "Mia will explain why after all the roses are handed out."

It had taken me a while to find chocolate roses so long after Valentine's Day. Finally, Mom had found a drug store that still had some, plus they were on clearance.

I came to Ashleigh and Alex before I'd expected it. They'd moved from where Alex had been sitting when we'd delivered roses on Valentine's Day. I stopped, a handful of roses in front of me, and stared at the two of them. They stared back.

"I'm sorry," I mouthed. I was looking at Ashleigh as I did so, but it went for Alex, too. Neither of them had spoken to me for the rest of the lock-in Friday, and of course, nobody had called me all weekend. That was fine with me, because it gave me more time to work on my plan.

Since neither of them responded, I set a rose on each desk and walked toward the front of the room, I tried to gather my courage. With each step, I felt like I was getting stronger. I could do this. I really could. I'd prepared for it all weekend because I had no other choice.

I had to explain everything. No more hiding. No more secrets.

But most importantly, no more games. My sister was great, but I was great too. It didn't matter if I received a hundred roses on Valentine's Day or none at all. What was important was really good friends, parents who were proud of me, and doing the right thing. When I'd been dishonest about the roses, it had been the wrong thing, even though I had good reasons for doing it. I realized that now.

I'd have to do this in every other seventh-grade classroom as well. One rose for each person, purchased out of my allowance savings, and a speech for every class. This would be the hardest, though, because this class had Ashleigh and Alex. If I could do this class, I could do the rest.

I turned and faced the class. "Last year we all sat by and watched as the same people collected roses," I began. "Do you know how it feels to sit by while everyone around you gets roses? You hope, maybe just this once, that one of those roses will come your way."

I looked at the people in front of me then and judged their reactions. I ignored Kaylee and her friends, and I didn't dare look in Ashleigh's direction. I'd lose all my nerve if I saw either her or Alex.

But there were plenty of other people to look at. They seemed to be hearing what I was saying and nodding. That gave me the push to go forward.

"So that was what I did," I continued. "I didn't think about what I was doing, I guess. It hurt people. I sent roses to people from secret admirers and let them figure out who had sent them. It was wrong."

"But you are setting it right," Ms. Phillips said. "And we thank you for that, don't we?"

I wasn't finished yet. I continued speaking.

"This will only set things right if you have the courage to do something," I said. "Most of you have crushes on someone you'd never, ever tell. Tell them. Take the chance."

People looked down. Out of the corner of my eye, I saw that Kaylee had that sneer on her face again.

"If you don't have a crush, write something nice to some-one," I continued. "Someone you'd never tell in person. And sign it. Sign your name to it. None of this secret admirer stuff."

"Thank you," Ms. Phillips said. She stepped forward and began giving everyone instructions, leaving me to step back. That was when I dared to make eye contact with Ashleigh. She smiled at me, and for the first time in days, I had hope.

Maybe my friends could forgive me.

"That will be all, Miss Hartley," Ms. Phillips said. "You're free to go to your next homeroom."

Ms. Phillips knew I was doing this in every seventh-grade classroom, so she was just trying to help. But I wanted to stay around and find out if Ashleigh and Alex really had forgiven me. With no other choice, though, I began walking around, collecting roses, as people wrote. I had to keep them separate from the blank cards or I'd have a mess.

Alex handed me his without looking at me, and my heart fell. My smile fell as well. I wanted to read his, but I knew that would be wrong, even if I did it after I got into the hallway.

Ashleigh was still writing. I'd passed her to pick up Alex's, but when I backed up, she kept writing like I wasn't even standing there. She held it up but didn't hand it over when I wrapped my fingers around it. Her gaze moved deliberately to the card, where I looked at it and saw the words, *Read this now.*

Maybe I was slow, but it took a second for me to realize that was meant for me. I opened the card, right there in front of everyone, and read the words I'd been hoping to read.

I'm sorry, she'd written. *Let's talk.*

I looked at her and nodded. She knew I was sorry as well. That was what this whole thing was about. But I mouthed the words, "I'm sorry too," just to make sure.

Then I turned and rolled the cart into the hallway, feeling better about things already. I still had to make things right with the rest of the school. One class down, the rest of the seventh-grade classrooms to go. The roses were just a way to help people the honest way this time.

At the end of homeroom, it was time to give the roses out. I set the cart in front of a table in the hallway, where I quickly realized I'd taken on far more than I could handle. How could I have ever thought one person could do all of this? I had to arrange everything alphabetically without reading the messages and then hand them out when people came to get theirs. And I had about five seconds to do it before final bell rang.

Final bell rang and I still had a mess. Students, who had all been told to come to the trophy case to get their roses, began lining up. I was still digging through cards, trying to find one for the first person in line, when I heard a voice behind me.

"I'll help you."

"Me too."

I turned around and there was Ashleigh. I smiled. Then I saw Alex standing behind her, and my smile widened. I was relieved they were helping me, sure, but mostly I was just relieved they were both my friends again.

"There's something I never told you," Ashleigh said, low enough so only I could hear. "I sent Kaylee's rose. I wanted to watch her try to figure out who sent it."

I was stunned. "Did you tell her?" I asked.

"I will," Ashleigh answered. "I want to help you first."

Sun and Gillianni pushed through the crowd behind Ashleigh. They were there to help too. Together, we handed out cards until the only ones that were left were the ones for each of us.

All of us had more than one. I personally had written up one for each of them, telling them what I thought was great about them, but I was surprised to find they'd all done the same. I saved Alex's for last, and once the rest of our friends had stepped off to the side to give us a few minutes alone, we read each other's.

I'd written him just a few simple words. *I was too naive to realize it before, but I've liked you for a long, long, long time.* His smile told me those had been the right words. Then he waited while I read mine.

You're the most amazing person I've ever known.

Ashleigh, Sun, and Gillianni had all written similar things. Even though they'd all gotten mad at me, when they'd stopped to think about it, they realized I'd been trying to do the right thing. Trying to help others. And now, by helping me, they were doing the right thing too.

I knew we still had a lot to talk about, but at least we were talking. As long as they'd let me make it up to them, I'd start today and make sure I never, ever broke my friends' trust again.

"So no more matchmaking?" Alex said as we started toward class after pushing the cart back to the principal's office.

"No way," I said. "Seventh graders are in charge of their own lives from now on. I'm just happy hanging out with my friends and being me."

He smiled at me. I smiled back. I couldn't believe it had taken me this long to realize how much I liked him. Even worse, he'd liked me all this time and I'd never even realized it. It looked like all that time I'd spent matchmaking, I almost missed what was right in front of me all along.

ACKNOWLEDGMENTS

Most people don't realize it takes a small village to create a book. I'm lucky to have the best village ever. Thank you to my agent, Natalie Lakosil; my editor, Alyson Heller; everyone at Simon & Schuster, especially Teresa Ronquillo; and my copyeditor, Valerie Shea.

Speaking of cheerleaders, a big thank-you to everyone who supported me in the release of my first book, including the Midsouth SCBWI, Mary Grey at Parnassus Books, and Sue at BookManBookWoman. I hope to bring many more readers your way!

I also have to thank the person in my junior high who brought in the carnation sale for Valentine's Day. Without that, I might not ever have been inspired to write about chocolate roses.

Thank you to my husband, Neil, who makes life so fun and amazing. I look forward to seeing where our adventure takes us next.